THE CAMINO KILLER

Eliot Locke Thrillers
Book Two

Dean Carson

SAPERE
BOOKS

THE CAMINO KILLER

Published by Sapere Books.

20 Windermere Drive, Leeds, England, LS17 7UZ,
United Kingdom

saperebooks.com

ISBN: 978-1-80055-141-1

PROLOGUE

Where any story begins is a bit of a philosophical conundrum. You could say this story began in the eleventh century, when the remains of an early saint were found in northern Spain. Or you could say it began in the nineties, when walking holidays became trendy. Or you could say it began five years ago, when a banker met an unfortunate end crucified under a bridge. But I like to think it began a few weeks ago, when I found myself looking down the dark barrel of a .22 Beretta 87 target pistol...

But let's go back a little earlier. To just short of a year ago, in the charming city of Burgos in Spain.

Dust motes danced in the Spanish air, sinuously rising and falling, keeping time with the beat coming from the jazz band forcing its way down the crowded street. Ben Cavendish, a 23-year-old recent law graduate, sat at the little metal table, crushed against the outer wall of the tavern, and grinned at his two companions. Six hours ago, he didn't know them at all. Now they were best friends, enjoying a wonderful adventure together.

That was the joy of the Camino Way. You meet someone, you like them, you are instant friends. You meet someone, you don't like them, you bend down to do up your shoelaces. When you pop back up they are in the distance, and you never see them again. If only life could be that simple.

They were sitting at a tiny table outside a crowded bar in the medieval city of Burgos, one of the great cities along the greatest pilgrim route in the world. The Camino de Santiago wends its way across 800 kilometres of northern Spain, from the border with France, across the Pyrenees, and on through Navarre, La Rioja, Castilla y Leon, before ending up close to the Atlantic coast in Galicia. Six weeks of blisters, penance, camaraderie and new friendships on Europe's most travelled walking route.

The bar was packed — a mix of locals and tourists. Many carried the dust of the trail in their hair. You could tell the walkers. They had a weary but happy look, and tired legs. No cares, but plenty of aches.

Ben stretched out his legs to ease the strain on his knees. He smiled. One of his new best friends might actually become a new best friend. She was gorgeous. And the band was coming closer. *There will be dancing.*

She was beside him now, tucking into her second plate of foie gras: lightly fried engorged livers of force-fed ducks and geese. He shuddered. As a vegan, this was normally a red line. But as a vegan, he wasn't in high demand in the dating game and couldn't be too choosy. He tried not to think of the poor duck. He tried instead to think of the lips devouring it's liver. Luscious lips. Plump juicy lips. Lips that might soon be on his lips, mashing into them. He would taste the cherry sweetness of her lipstick, and feel her tongue dance the devil's tango with his own, and taste ... and taste the bloody engorged livers of dead birds.

He scowled.

And then she looked at him and winked.

To hell with ducks and geese.

He would follow his carnal desires and see where they led.

The jazz band was bravely battling its way up the street, swaying to the rhythms it created. A group of young Spanish men dressed in bright blue shirts followed it, dancing in the narrow canyon between high buildings on each side. It was a stag party. And the street was coming alive with the revelry.

Then the sound of a second band, low in the distance, began to rumble through the air. Heavier on the percussion, it sounded like African *tom tom* drums to Ben. It only took a few minutes, but the second band turned the corner and joined the melee in front of him. This second band was followed by a large group of women, all wearing pink T-shirts. One of the women also wore a white veil, and had a big red L plate on her back. The bride-to-be.

When both groups met in the middle of the street, the two bands morphed seamlessly into the same tune, and the pink shirts and the blue shirts began to pair off and dance. It didn't take long before people stood up from their tables, leaving their drinks and plates of tapas, and joined in the fun.

Megan — no surname, he hadn't asked — looked across at Ben and smiled. Her hand stretched across the table and touched his, and he felt a thrill of electricity surge through him.

To hell with the fat ducks.

He grinned foolishly. He stood and bowed formally towards her. She got up and smiled at him, the hint of something mischievous twinkling in her eyes. She returned his bow, and they turned, hand in hand, towards the street.

Just then there was a slight plopping sound, and Ben looked at her, puzzled. He looked back towards the table, and saw that something had landed in his beer. He frowned and looked up briefly. Had someone dropped something from one of the upper floors, or had some bit of detritus dropped from one of the hanging baskets?

He let go of Megan's hand and bent to look into his beer, then recoiled in horror. Floating in the glass was a human finger, jagged bone protruding where it was severed from the rest of the hand.

Megan followed his gaze and saw the floating digit. "It's a fake, you eejit," she said, her soft Irish brogue taking the edge off the words. "Someone is pranking you." She reached into the glass and pulled out the finger. Her face registered disgust. "It's bloody realistic," she said.

She looked up, and she saw what Ben had missed. Protruding from one of the flower boxes on the second floor was a severed human arm, still pink and fleshy, but horribly swollen and blotchy. Flies were buzzing around it.

Megan opened her mouth wide and screamed, as a speck of blood fell from the sky and splattered onto the table.

ONE

I was pissed off. A job is a job, but even hitmen deserve to be treated with some respect. Perhaps hitmen more than any other class of employee; our ultimate sanction against a bad boss is not to go on strike but to strike with lethal efficiency. And whoever was employing me right now was getting on my goat. Industrial relations were sinking to an all-time low. His days were becoming numbered.

It had begun alright, I suppose. The usual way — an offer of a job on the Magic Bistro website.

Don't go looking for the Magic Bistro. You will be disappointed. It is a specialist website for magicians, and unless you are a card flicker, you just won't be interested. It's the real thing. The nerd who set it up is an actual amateur magician. And amateur is the right word. I have seen him perform. He is a dreadful bore. He always reminds me of a quotation from Somerset Maugham: "He asked me if I liked card tricks. I said no. He did six."

But what most of his magical friends don't know is that the boring accountant who does boring card tricks is actually a forensic accountant, and he works for the CIA. And for those of us in the know, the Magic Bistro serves a completely different purpose. It is the front for a forum of hitmen.

I had logged onto the Bistro a few days earlier and saw a Spanish magician was selling a set of Rice Bowls. Google them. Your grandfather might have been impressed by the trick. I doubt you would be.

But I knew the hidden meaning. Someone was looking for a person to be killed, in Spain. And I was looking to escape the rain and wind of Edinburgh. It was a natural match.

I put in a bid on the item and got it. Or, in plain terms, I was hired to carry out the hit. I was the only bidder, which probably meant the hirer was looking specifically for me. It happens. Reputations matter, even in the most murky and secretive world.

That was why I found myself flying into Biarritz.

Which was why I was so pissed off.

My instructions were clear. When I landed, there would be a message on the Bistro telling me where to go. I stared at the message and felt my blood pressure rising.

"Take the bus to St Jean Pied de Port, and await instructions."

I don't take buses, and I hate treasure hunts almost as much as I hate card tricks.

And I hate buses even more. No leg room. But I took the bus to St Jean Pied de Port, and put up with the discomfort of having my legs folded like pretzels. An hour and a half later, we arrived. Then I logged onto the Bistro and got the next message.

"Go to the Pilgrim Passport office and get your Pilgrim Passport. Tomorrow morning, walk to the monastery of Roncesvalles, where the cardinal will meet you."

That's when I got really pissed off.

The abbey at Roncesvalles is almost thirty kilometres from St Jean, across a Pyrenean Pass that rises higher than Ben Nevis.

I hate cardinals even more than I hate buses, and I hate walking even more than I hate cardinals. It was going to be one of those jobs. If I took it. They were already making me earn my money, and the job hadn't even begun.

I caught my first break as I was cursing under my breath at the bus stop.

"First Camino?"

I turned with a scowl, but managed to twist my mouth up into a grimace with the semblance of a smile. A young lady who had been on the bus with me was smiling back at me. I let her. She was slim with eyes like sloes, and hair like dark chocolate. Just my type. Any woman who will talk to me is my type. In that, I am like most men.

"I came by accident," I muttered.

"Many do," she said enigmatically. "Are you doing the full distance?"

I didn't know much about the Camino, but I knew it was 800 kilometres long. So no, I wasn't doing the full distance. Did I look like a moron? But some part of me knew this was the wrong answer. So I smiled back.

"We'll see," I said. "I'm Paul."

That was the name I was travelling under at the moment: Paul Vandy. An Edwardian magician and juggler. It's one of my little foibles. I like to use the names of old variety artists and magicians for my fake documentation.

"Liz," she replied.

I assumed it was her real name. I went with the flow rather than cutting off the conversation. It wasn't that I fancied her. I am not in the relationship business. My last one had ended badly when my girlfriend tried to stab me while we were relaxing on a boat in Venice. We haven't talked since. I left her behind and came home. I presume she is still there — I had wrapped enough chain around her body.

So I wasn't interested in Liz. But it does no harm to keep in flirting practice. You never know…

Liz took me under her wing, and the next hour passed pleasantly. We walked up a steep hill and went into a small stone building in the lee of a squat medieval church. This, apparently, was the passport office. I was travelling under a perfectly good passport, which a friend in Miami had got me for doing him a favour. The Pilgrim passport was a lot less official than my Paul Vandy one — just a flimsy sheet of card, folded lengthwise four times. But according to Liz, it would prove invaluable over the coming days. Present it at a hostel and sleep for under a tenner. Or get a pilgrim dinner for a pittance. Without the Pilgrim passport, you were condemned to five star hotels and good restaurants. The horror...

Darkness was descending when we finally left the office. We grabbed a pizza, then Liz suggested we try a hostel before they filled up. I would have preferred a hotel, but apparently the job I had taken required me to pass for a pilgrim, so I went along with her suggestion. But I chalked it up as one more black mark against the cardinal.

The first three hostels were full, and I was just contemplating a night under the stars when we spotted a tiny sign over a door, and we knocked. It was a private hostel, and they had three beds left in a mixed dorm. We snapped up two. I got the top bunk. I was about to joke about preferring my women on top, but realised that in a room full of pilgrims perhaps keeping my mouth shut was the better option. We said our goodnights, and I retired to the comfort of my dingy blanket.

And then — the lights went out! Strict curfew at ten.

I woke the following morning at six, not by choice but because everyone else in the dormitory woke at six. By seven, everyone was on the road, rising towards the distant hills. It looked like a publicity still for *The Sound of Music*. All that was missing were the singing nuns.

I let them go ahead and got breakfast. Then, instinct kicking in, I slipped a sharp fruit knife into my sock, holding it in place with a spare lace. I don't know why I did that. It was uncomfortable during the walk, and almost useless as a weapon. But I am a hitman, and I was unarmed. I feel more naked without a weapon than I do without pants.

The walk wasn't as bad as I expected, aside from the walking part and the feel of the knife rubbing against my calf. The company was good. Liz was a long way in the distance, but I fell in step with a surprising number of interesting people. Not the God-botherers I was expecting, but thoughtful, interesting sorts. Everyone had a story, and some of the stories were worth hearing. They whiled away the time.

The first hour was spent on gentle country roads. After that, we moved onto rolling countryside and farm tracks. Two hours in, I stopped for a sandwich. I asked for a salami baguette, and that is exactly what I got. A baguette with a stump of salami in it. No butter or sauce, no salad, no cheese. Hungry rations.

By midday we were nearing the top of the Napoleon Pass, called that because the Little Corporal had passed this way. With an army. Why he didn't take the low road is beyond me. Just before the Napoleon Pass plunges from the road into the trees, there was a large catering truck, and I stopped for a coffee. Liz was just getting up from a low wall, but she paused for a moment.

"The worst is over," she said. "Just over the pass, then down to Roncesvalles. Most of it is through forest. Just be careful not to lose the path. At one point it dips sharply downhill, but most people just keep going straight. Don't worry if you miss the turn; but it adds an hour to your walk."

And then she was gone.

I left the blacktop to cross a series of fields, gently rising towards woods. The crowd had thinned out. The fitter were already near the end of their day's march. The fatter were behind me. I was stuck in the middle, in street shoes. And I was carrying a suitcase. No one had told me about a 30 kilometre hike, and my feet were beginning to blister. That cardinal would get a piece of my mind when I finally got to the monastery.

The line of travellers was really strung out when I parted some strands of barbed wire and ducked under them. The path turned to mud, and I realised I could not see the people ahead. I stole a glance behind, and was alone from that side too. At this altitude it was getting cold. I felt a chill like a gnarly finger scratching across my soul, but I brushed it aside. Ever since reading *Lord of the Rings* as a child, I have had a thing about forests and spiders. But it was all in my head. Ignoring my foreboding, I plunged onto the dark path. I even snapped a spider's web, just to say I didn't care.

TWO

It wasn't as bad as I feared. The path was about six feet wide, bordered on each side by dense, high trees. The centre of the path was a strip of mud, churned up by the countless pilgrim boots that had passed this way since the spring thaw. It would have been pleasant walking if I had been in boots. Instead, I had to stick to the grass and weed verge, because every time my feet strayed into the centre of the path they sank, and a wave of mud squelched over the top and soaked into my socks.

And I was getting thoroughly sick of the suitcase swinging by my side. My arm felt like it was being dragged out of my shoulder socket. No matter how fit the gym gets you — and I am a workout machine — nothing prepares you for thirty kilometres over rough ground swinging a suitcase. There is a reason armies march with a rucksack.

The trail wound steeply uphill, then levelled out for a while. The gloom was oppressive, occasionally relieved by a gleam of sun through the high foliage or by the sounds of birds. At every rustle I imagined the pad of giant spider legs.

At one point, I spotted a field mouse right in the middle of the mud path. I stopped and bent down to get a better view, and he froze, allowing me a good look. It was only after I walked on that it occurred to me he was probably stuck in the mud and I should have carried him to the verge. But I wasn't going back for a mouse. My objection to collateral damage on a mission does not extend to the wildlife.

The path was easy to follow. There were few turn-offs, and at each one there was always an arrow to indicate the correct way. I was beginning to get used to the strange bushcraft of the Camino. The arrows were always either painted in yellow, or the indicator contained some version of a scallop shell. Yellow and scallops must be symbols of the pilgrimage, I supposed. Perhaps the first man through this way had eaten a bad shellfish, and the colour and shape had stuck all this time?

The fact that I was even speculating about such things should have told me my mind was drifting and I was losing the sense of awareness that had kept me alive for so many years. But what could happen out here?

After a particularly steep section, the path swept to the right. I was just sweeping to the right with it when something caught my eye. A stump at the side of the road was daubed with a crude yellow arrow. And it did not point to the right. It pointed down a narrow cleft in the forest, running sharply to the left and downhill.

This was a surprise, and I stopped for a moment, contemplating both paths. The path to the right was wide and muddy. Many boots had passed this way. The path to the left was less defined and rougher. It was also narrower and the ground was grassy. Far fewer feet had trodden it.

Clearly the yellow arrow had been moved by some joker. But as I looked down the narrow path, I spotted a cockle shell tied to a low hanging branch. And a little further on, gleaming in a rare patch of sunlight, rosary beads twinkled. So pilgrims had passed down this way. Was this the easy-to-miss shortcut that would take an hour off my day?

Perhaps the main path was a farmer's track or a right of way. The narrow path seemed to be the pilgrim one, and so I plunged boldly to the left and began descending.

Almost instantly all my misgivings vanished. The path was not muddy. I could walk down the centre without my socks taking a pounding from the ooze. This was an improvement.

The path was narrow, though. Not many pilgrims had passed, or if they had they had been careful to leave no trace of their passing. And I noticed it was eerily quiet. Not even the chirping of the woodland birds, or the menacing march of the spiders.

I walked on. I'm a big boy, and it takes more than a spooky wood to put me off my game. There were no spiders here.

Then I spotted it. A small slash gleamed in a shard of sunlight streaming from the forest canopy. A straight white line, like a wire. A bloody cobweb.

Did I mention I hate spiders? Not a phobia, or anything. I just don't like them. If they had necks I would wring the scrawny things. And this spider must be seriously big, because the line of his web was long and straight. I followed it to a tree, then around the tree.

That was the clue. True spider web is made from a sort of gummy silk that protrudes from the arse of a spider when it is in DIY mode. It doesn't run around trees or branches. It sticks to them.

Something was not right, and the instinctive reptilian part of my brain cottoned on to it quicker than my intellect. It looked like a wire because it was a wire.

I dropped into a squat, moving slightly off-trail into the undergrowth.

Nothing to be alarmed about. Lots of reasons you would find a wire in a wood. It could have been part of a fence. It might have come from an underwire bra, after the fabric rotted away in the open. Though she must have been a Godzilla of a woman to have needed that much underwire. The most likely explanation was that it was a snare, designed to trap small animals.

I was about to move forward to check it out when a twig snapped behind me. I instantly froze, trying to make myself small against the weeds and vegetation.

Almost imperceptibly I lowered my suitcase to the ground to free up both my hands. The forest was silent as a graveyard. I waited.

Seconds passed.

Minutes passed.

I waited…

I knew it was safe. It had to be safe. But amateurs move when it is safe. And amateurs die. I waited.

A full five minutes passed, but it felt like fifty. My legs were aching from the crouch, the muscles screaming at me. I felt a dull ache in my back.

Then a rustle.

It was a slight rustle. It could have been a small animal moving in the bushes. It could have been the wind swaying the boughs. But it wasn't.

The sound was slight, and intermittent. But it was moving closer to me by the moment. I raised my head slightly and rolled my shoulders, to give the impression I was no longer on alert.

The rustling got closer. And closer.

And then it stopped.

When it was clear that the rustling had stopped permanently rather than just pausing, I began to count off the seconds in my head.

Thirty-eight seconds into my count, the bushes behind me exploded into noise.

And instantly I straightened and lay out flat, rolling rapidly along the ground. I rolled towards the noise, not away from it.

That is what saved my life.

As I rolled, the forest and the sky forming a kaleidoscope of images, I saw a man straighten up and run towards me, swinging a vicious metal cosh. The cosh was raised high over his shoulder, and he brought it down in a tight arc right for where my head had been.

He didn't have time to recover. Had I rolled away, he might have hit me on the shoulder, back or leg, and that would have hurt. But I rolled towards him, flat on the ground. I was well below the arc of his swing, and well inside it.

His leg caught my hip, and he fell headlong to the ground. But he was good; he rolled and managed to end up sitting, facing towards me.

It gave me the second I needed, and I reached for a rock I had spotted nearby. My fingers closed on the rough stone, and I yanked it.

It didn't move. It was stuck. In that moment I lost my advantage, and he was on me.

I rolled away from his first crude blow, but the cosh clipped my shoulder and numbed it. I was fighting one-handed. With my left, never my good side.

Before I could scramble to my feet he was on me, pinning me to the ground. The cosh — about a foot long, covered in leather — rose high, ready for the strike.

Then I remembered the butter knife. I twisted. He tried to pull me back into position, but the movement was enough to free my leg. I brought my ankle up until I could reach it with my left hand, and I wrenched the fruit knife free. I slashed it viciously across his forearm, raking the sharp edge through his yielding flesh. He screamed in agony as the rough blade lacerated the skin and tore into his tendons. A spray of arterial blood slashed across my face and neck. It felt hot. The cosh fell harmlessly from his grip, hitting me on the forehead as it bounced to the ground. Damn — that would bruise.

I jerked my body up and heaved at him with my good hand. He fell over backwards, and I staggered to my feet.

I had dropped the knife, and I lost a second glancing around for it. I should have just gone for him with my hands. But he too had staggered to his feet.

Instead of facing me, he turned down the path and plunged through the vegetation, crashing down the hill with all the grace of an elephant doing the tango.

I set off in pursuit, but my usual awareness had deserted me in the adrenalin rush of the fight. I forgot the wire — until a sharp pain in my lead leg brought it back to my mind. I went down hard.

Someone upstairs must have been watching me. I have an agreement with God. I don't believe in him, and he doesn't believe in me. But he must have broken his rule, because my hand landed just inches from a vicious animal trap. Not one designed to catch and hold an animal, but one whose edges were serrated. Had the trap closed on my hand, the teeth would have done far more than break bones. Looking at the jaws of hell, I sighed in relief, then got up and followed my quarry more cautiously. I was not going to fall victim to any more booby traps.

But he was now fifty metres clear of me, and moving faster than me. Either he knew where the traps were, or he was throwing caution to the wind.

The path didn't improve. He was drawing clear of me. As a schoolboy I had been forced to race cross-country, but it had never been like this.

There was a break in the trees, and he ran into a field. The distance between us was now nearly eighty metres. There are two ways of catching someone. The first is to run like the clappers and hope you are faster than them. That falls down because after a couple of hundred metres you are completely knackered, and they dance off into the sunset while you collapse at the side of the trail and wait for the ambulance with the oxygen supply.

The second way is to keep a steady pace and gradually close the distance, hoping they will be the one to collapse at the side of the road, and you will reach them before the ambulance revives them. That was my strategy. Halfway across the field I had closed the distance back to fifty metres and was gaining steadily.

He vaulted a gate, and was onto a country road. I vaulted the gate and chased. Forty metres. Thirty-five.

Suddenly, there was a roaring sound behind me. Without breaking stride, I turned and saw a powerful motorbike swooping down the country road. Aimed right at me.

I dived into the ditch and watched as the bike sped past, the dust cloud clogging my screaming lungs.

The bike slowed, my attacker clambered onto the back, and they disappeared in a haze of smoke. *Damn*!

THREE

I took my time getting back on the trail. I caught my breath, scanned the surrounding countryside for more assassins, then scoured the scene of the fight for any clues as to what the hell had happened. It all took time.

It was obvious that the place had been set up as an attack zone, but by amateurs. Apparently, I had been meant to stumble over the tripwire and hit the ground, at which point my attacker would spring from hiding and jump me. The animal traps — there were two of them — were put there more in hope than in expectation. A sort of ineffectual afterthought.

If I was a cop, I'm sure I could have found something useful. But I'm not a cop. Don't particularly like them as a species. So I didn't bother with a forensic sweep for clues. I regained the trail, and took a moment to remove the rosary beads and cockle shells from the side trail, and to re-point the yellow arrow. I even pulled across some vegetation to make the side trail look less inviting.

I was sure the two would not return that day, but they would probably be out again tomorrow to prey on more innocent pilgrims. Though looking at the pilgrims I had met, I thought it was slim pickings.

That done, I set off up the trail, which continued for another two kilometres before levelling out, and for another four kilometres before showing any signs of descending. My shoes were pinching, my suitcase was dragging, and I was really eager to meet this cardinal. I was going to wring his bloody neck.

Finally I reached the crest of the pass and looked down the verdant valley to the monastery of Roncesvalles, nestling beside a small river in a grove of beech trees. Only four kilometres away, but the descent was over rocky ground through dense woods. Ideal ground to rip up the last of my street shoes.

It took an hour. As I crossed a small bridge to the meadow in front of the abbey, I spotted four middle-aged Irish men sitting in their jocks in the river. How could I tell they were Irish? Partly it was the pasty bodies, but the real giveaway was that I had met them several hours earlier when they charged past me at the start of the first incline. They waved cheerfully. I smiled back. My smile did not reach my eyes.

When I walked into the reception, a snooty woman told me not to lean up against the desk. I have killed people for less.

"I'm here to meet the cardinal," I muttered.

"This is a monastery. The man in charge is the abbot."

"I don't care whether it is abbot, costello, or the monster. I want to see Cardinal Benoluchi."

She looked at me blankly. I could see that she was thinking of calling security. Do monasteries have security?

"There is no cardinal staying here tonight," she said eventually.

The impasse was resolved when a tall man with a pleasant smile walked over and tapped me on the shoulder. He smiled apologetically.

"His Eminence is travelling incognito. If you'd like to get your bed and take a shower, I can bring you to him then."

"That works for me," I said. "But what works better is that you bring me to him now."

I followed him down a stone corridor and through a door marked *Private — Community Only*. Obviously the clerical portion of the huge building. The smell of stale feet and stale clothing decreased dramatically. The ache in my feet did not decrease, and I realised I needed a drink and a carb hit. I was exhausted. I am a fit man, but I had not been prepared for today, and it would take a few hours to return to my usual self.

So I walked into the cardinal's quarters ready for a fight.

I was a bit surprised at his lack of luxury. Cardinals are the princes of the Church, and normally they live a life commensurate with that status. I don't know quite what I was expecting — perhaps a golden throne and a manservant in a priest's collar hovering at his shoulder. Instead, I found a small room with a simple canteen table and two chairs. Not even a table cloth. A man in his late fifties or early sixties, who could have been my accountant if hitmen paid taxes, was seated at the table reading a newspaper. He was dressed in a black pants and black shirt, but with no tell-tale white collar. If it wasn't for the ornate silver crucifix, with rubies, hanging from a thick chain around his neck, I would have passed him without a second glance. The crucifix was impressive, though — probably seventeenth century, from my limited knowledge of antiques. Probably worth more than my car, or my Barrett's M50 sniper rifle. He pimped up well.

I sat down opposite him. He smiled.

"Do I call you Your Majesty, Your Highness, or what?"

"Your Eminence is the normal form of address, but I think Fermin will do perfectly. You must be Eliot Locke?"

We shook hands. His grip was warm and firm. At least he was not standing on ceremony. I was too tired for that shit.

"I use the name Paul Vandy for operational purposes," I pointed out.

"Yes. You mentioned that in the messages, Eliot. How did you find the journey?" he went on.

I looked at him like he had donkey ears, but did my best to be polite. He didn't understand the importance of security.

"Delightful," I said. "But you'll forgive me if I am anxious to just cut to the chase. I've been walking all day, and I am full of no dinner."

"Forgive me," he murmured, and tapped the glass in front of him with his knife. The tinkle echoed in the small room, and almost immediately a monk emerged from a side door and placed a bowl of steaming soup in front of me, and another in front of the cardinal. It smelt delicious. It was a simple garlic and chickpea soup thickened, I found out later, with stale bread. A 600 year tradition on the Camino, and surprisingly tasty. I ignored the cardinal while I dealt with the soup, and felt better when I shovelled the last mouthful past my grateful tongue.

As we waited for the next course, he said: "We do have a job for you. A job for someone of your special talents. But we can discuss it over coffee. Let's enjoy our dinner first."

And for the next thirty minutes I got a potted history of the monastery, Napoleon and his crossing of the Pyrenees, and the Camino. Interesting stuff, and the cardinal told his stories well. It helped that the second course was a slow-cooked half duck in a rich red wine reduction.

"I wonder what the poor suckers getting the pilgrim meal are being fed," I joked.

"The same as us," he replied seriously. "Three courses and half a bottle of red wine per person. We are all equal on this pilgrimage."

"So did you walk here?"

He grinned. "Some of us are more equal than others — though I have walked it in the past. Interesting story — this room is used for people like me, who book in advance and don't sleep in the pilgrim dorms. Martin Sheen slept in it."

I looked at him blankly. I had heard of Martin Sheen, an American-Mexican actor who starred in some dreadful Vietnam movie in the seventies. I couldn't see him walking the Camino, but with his Mexican heritage he was probably Catholic, so you never know.

The cardinal went on: "When he was filming *The Way*, his son's movie about the Camino." He sighed in mock exasperation. "You must be the only person on the walk who hasn't seen that movie." He took a sip of his wine. "Keep it that way — it was a snore-fest."

The dessert was the first sour note of the meal, an undistinguished almond tart. But the coffee that followed was pungent and sharp. I sighed appreciatively.

The cardinal pushed aside his coffee cup and placed a leather satchel on the table between us. "Down to business." He looked across the table and me, and his eyes were suddenly steely. "I need you to hunt down a man."

FOUR

I raised an eyebrow. "You know what I do for a living?"

He brushed it aside dismissively. "I don't want him killed. I want him hunted down, and stopped."

"You better start at the beginning."

So he did.

It had started five years previously. A German woman walking the Camino had disappeared on the second stage; from the monastery at Roncesvalles to the village of Zubiri. Her travelling companion reported her missing the following morning. She had assumed the missing woman had walked ahead, as they were walking at different speeds.

"Common enough among friends who do the pilgrimage together," the cardinal assured me. "They often set out together but walk at their own pace, meeting for lunch and in the evenings. That's why the woman didn't panic immediately."

The search had been extensive, but the missing woman had not been found. She had not gone on; she had not gone home. She was not on the trail. Eventually, the search was scaled down. Then it was called off.

"We didn't suspect anything out of the ordinary," said the cardinal. "People drop out to escape bad marriages and other situations. Sometimes they drop out permanently — walk into a river with stones in their pockets. Tragic, but what can you do?" He shrugged expressively.

I shrugged back at him. I felt like I was in a pantomime.

He shrugged again. This was getting silly.

"So what happened?" I asked.

"Four months after she disappeared, her body was found. In a river. But she hadn't gone in voluntarily. Her body had been drained totally of blood, and she was wired to the central arch of the Puente de la Rabia, in Zubiri, like she had been crucified upside down."

He opened the leather satchel and pulled out a photo, sliding it across the table. I looked. The image was a bit cluttered, but there was no mistaking the upside down crucifixion.

"Like St Peter."

He seemed surprised that I knew that. "I suppose a bit like St Peter. That's odd. Her name was Petronella. She was a journalist who had written many articles condemning the Church, and she was a very public face of atheism. We wondered if that was a factor in her death."

I looked at him, puzzled.

"Oh, you know," he said. "St Peter denied Christ three times in the garden of Gethsemane. And he ended up crucified upside down. She denied Christ, and she ended up crucified upside down."

"A bit of a stretch," I muttered.

"I thought so too," said the cardinal. "Until we had a second killing a year later. An investment banker, part of a venture capitalist group that took over the mortgages of a failing bank, and evicted hundreds of homeowners in Ireland. The guy was painted all over in gold paint, and suffocated."

"That's a myth. Painting someone in gold doesn't cause them to suffocate. We don't breathe through the skin. Just ask any human statue you see busking."

"Technically, the banker did not die of suffocation. The fiend who painted him put a poison in the paint, and it gradually paralysed all the muscles, including those involved in breathing. The banker died in agony over a number of hours, according to the police. His body was left on the altar at the Cathedral of Astorga in the evening, and found the following morning. He was alive when he was put on the altar, but the poison took him over the hours of darkness."

"Wow," I muttered, and I looked at the second photo the cardinal slid across to me. It was taken in the church, and the flash gave a weird pallor to the golden banker. His face was contorted in agony. That was hardcore, even for me. I have known some sick bastards — hazard of my profession — but that was a new level of cruelty.

"The following year, there was a third death. This time, it was a female barrister who had argued for the release of a paedophile priest. She lied in court, and her punishment was to have her mouth sewn shut. She had starved to death, in a cellar full of food."

I looked at the third picture, an anonymous face on a morgue slab. Her lips were sutured together with crude medical stitches, pulling her haunted features into a creepy grin.

"Harsh. Something biblical about that."

"The Bible I follow is a Bible of love," objected the cardinal. "This sick prick is working from his own book."

It was a bit of a shock to hear a man of the cloth swearing. My eyes must have betrayed it.

"Sorry," he said. "But I am up to my ears in this. At first we thought it was just bad luck, a few murders on the Camino. It has happened in the past. But one every year? No, something is going on. By the third, we suspected that the same person was behind them. Then came last year."

He paused to collect his thoughts, and poured himself a glass of wine. He knocked it back, then poured another.

"Last year was tough. I was put in charge of a special Church task force to keep an eye on the situation, so I was a bit too close to the action. It might be different for you, but I never come across murder at my desk job in the Vatican."

I shrugged. No point in telling a man of the cloth just how familiar I am with people who have ceased to be in very violent circumstances. Often circumstances of my making. I nodded sympathetically so that he would carry on.

"It was horrible. The victim last year was Herman Dahl."

I looked at him blankly.

"He ran the Dhal clinic in Bonn."

Something was vaguely coming back to me, but I shook my head. Let him do the memory work.

"He was all over the news a few years back when he got caught in that organ donor scandal. He was paying poor students from Eastern Europe and Asia for kidneys, for rich European recipients. Not strictly illegal, but it should be. A very dark and twisted thing to do. He was last year's victim."

"Last year's victim?" I asked. "You make it sound like this is a regular occurrence, an annual event."

He nodded sadly. "That seems to be the case. According to the police, we have a serial killer targeting pilgrims, taking one each year. Their deaths are always symbolic. A denier of Christ is crucified upside down. A moneylender is suffocated in gold. A liar has her lips sewn closed. Someone who cut up bodies had their own body cut up."

He held his head in his hands and sighed.

"The first part of Dhal's body was found when a hand fell on a group of people eating their dinner in Burgos. Over the next three days, body parts began appearing all over the region, each one on the Camino. At first we thought there were several victims. But when we put the parts together, we found that there was just one body. Or most of it, at least. The viscera never showed up, and the penis had been chopped off. And two fingers were missing, though we think an animal scavenged those."

He reached towards the satchel for another picture, but thought better of it.

"And the eyeballs," he added as an afterthought. His skin had gone grey as he recalled the incident.

I leaned back and looked at him carefully. "And you want me to hunt the killer?"

FIVE

"You know I am not a detective?" I asked.

"I know exactly what you are." There was sudden steel in his voice, but no hostility.

He reached into the leather satchel and removed a brown envelope, pushing it across the table towards me.

"5,000 euro. It is yours whether you help us or not. A payment for your time so far. And for the blisters you got on the journey." He smiled urbanely. "I know you are not a detective, but please hear me out. We have the whole Spanish police force hunting for this killer. They might find him. Stranger things have happened than Spanish efficiency. Your job is to stand behind the police, and catch him if they miss him."

"And to…?"

"God, no. Not to kill him. What do you think we are? On this mission, you are a bounty hunter — no more. We want him alive to face justice."

"But if it gets messy?"

The cardinal smiled enigmatically. "We will deal with that if it happens. But I have faith in you, my son."

I grinned. We were coming down to brass tacks now. "I see just one problem. As I said, I am no detective. If the police miss him, then I will miss him. Nothing is more certain."

The cardinal took a sip of his wine. "We have a plan," he said. "A very clever plan, if I may say so. We set a trap, we use a human bait; when he comes for the bait, you pounce."

I looked at him in stunned surprise. I could not have been more gobsmacked if someone had suggested we toss breadcrumbs on a village pond in the hope a great white shark might leap up and land in our net. Had this guy any conception of how the real world worked?

"You are sceptical."

Damn straight I was sceptical.

"Let me explain. The police have profilers. The Vatican has some of the best psychologists in the world. We know a lot about this killer. We know his mojo, what makes him tick."

A misuse of the word mojo, but I let it slide.

"He is punishing sinners, with deaths appropriate to their sins. One killing every year, always during the last two weeks of June." He saw the look of surprise on my face. "Yes, the killer takes his work holidays in June, and leaves his wife and family — the profilers tell us he has a wife and family — and he comes on the Camino. And he kills for kicks. It is June 16 now, and he is stalking our pilgrim paths as we speak. But we are ready for him. We have baited the trap." He had a triumphant, slightly mad, look in his eyes. "We have found him the perfect victim. Magda Lynn. You have heard of Magda Lynn?"

Who hadn't heard of her? Me, for one. I shook my head.

He looked surprised. "She is very well known. A charming lady, Polish I believe. She is, how you say, an adult actress. A filmic fornicator. She won two AVN awards last year."

Somewhere in the back of my head, I remembered that the Vatican was reputed to have the largest porn collection in the world. I had believed it to be ancient porn, but from the way this cleric was talking, they were bang up to date.

"I have not seen her movies myself, you understand," the cardinal continued. "I had a seminarian watch them and report back to me."

One lost vocation, I thought. But I kept that thought to myself. There were too many obvious jokes that sprang to mind, but I am better than that. At least I am when I am sober. After a few whiskies, I will take my shots with the best.

"Ms Lynn had asked the archdiocese for permission to make one of her movies on the Camino. I surprised her by saying yes."

He sat back with a smug look on his face. I waited. He went on.

"It will not be one of those pornographic movies she does, not this one. She is fronting a documentary about the Camino. The story of a fallen woman coming on pilgrimage to find her way back to God. Away from the vile world of sex on camera. That's what she said, and I said yes. But I told her that we would have our own person on the crew to keep an eye on things. That was part of the conditions of giving her permission. She would have to accept a minder."

"And she agreed?"

"Oh yes, in a heartbeat. A charming woman, but a bit gauche, if you know what I mean. I believe you will like her, though. A character, and a woman with a good heart, even if you have to dig deep to find it. If you take the job, you become her minder. Then we leak to the press that a porn actress is on the Camino. She is just the sort of victim our killer likes. So he comes for her."

"And I kill him?"

"No — you do not understand still. No killing. If the police capture him, you don't need to do anything at all except pass Go and collect your money. But if they fail, then you capture him."

"And will the police agree to this?"

He looked embarrassed. "They don't really know. They think you are just security hired to protect Miss Lynn. It was my idea to have you as a backup. In this part of the world Mother Church still has influence, so they agreed to let us bring in our own security expert — namely you."

He perked up slightly.

"You will have one ally on the force. Inspector Rodriguez is a religious man, a member of Opus Dei, and he has a slight suspicion that you are more than a bodyguard. He is one of us, though." The priest crossed himself surreptitiously. "So he is on board."

"Have you actually told him what you want me to do?"

"Of course not," said the cardinal, but I didn't know whether I believed him. He looked at me carefully. "Are you a Catholic?"

"Not even close," I admitted.

"A pity," he said. "If you were of the faith, I could have given you an indulgence if you had heard mass in Santiago at the end of your mission. A sort of get out of purgatory free card."

I looked at him blankly.

"If you had to kill him in the end, we could have forgiven you in advance. But we can't do that, so you have to take him alive."

The pressure was on.

SIX

The next day I met her — the bait. My brother Lester is a great one for cliches, and his words popped into my head: *Don't judge a book by the cover.* Magda was not what I had expected.

I expected a pneumatic blonde, probably about five foot nothing, with breasts so horribly humongous they'd cast a shadow that sucked the light out of the room. I expected aggressive yellow hair, enough of it to thatch a small roof, and the teeth of a young horse. Instead, Magda was a slim brunette. She was tall and willowy, dressed in a mid-length black skirt and a black sleeveless blouse. Admittedly the neckline of the blouse plunged a bit, and the breasts that reposed there like two contented kittens were a little larger and firmer than her slim frame might have indicated. But even the best surgeon can't make pop-ups look fully natural.

In a conservative business suit or a frumpy coat, she could have disappeared in a crowd. In a flame-red dress or a bikini, she could have turned heads so fast she would have caused whiplash.

An actor needs to be a chameleon, able to blend in. I am a bit like that myself, able to blend in as the occasion calls. But the difference is that the only time I turn heads is when I catch them perfectly on the point of the jaw with a well-timed hook.

"Magda," she said, offering a narrow graceful hand. I didn't know whether to shake it or kiss it. Luckily, Magda turned out to be a talker, and she gushed on before I had to decide.

"You must be my bodyguard? Is it like that film, you know, the Whitney Houston one? Do we fall madly for each other?"

"You tell me," I said. "Do you tend to fall for your leading men?"

I was joking, but her answer surprised me. She paused, and thought about it for a moment. "I think I do, a little bit. It makes the sex so much hotter. Doing it with someone you don't have a connection with is so hollow, and I think that comes out in the final performance. So yes, I do try to find something in each one of them, and I do try to feel a little bit of love."

I raised an eyebrow.

She went on: "Take you, for instance. I could fall for your gorgeous eyes. Or your broad shoulders. You have a lovely smile, but I suspect you are sparing with it. And there is a slight air of intellectual detachment about you. Are you a thinker, Eliot?"

But before I could answer, she carried on: "I like thinkers. I was going to major in history before I got diverted into the acting profession."

Acting? So that was how she saw it.

"It's not Eliot, it's Paul," I said, trying to bring the conversation back on track.

"The cardinal explained the name thing to me, Eliot," she said. Then she plunged on with her story, oblivious.

Over the next few minutes, the whole story came out. The early love of sex, the first appearances in a lap dancing club to pay the college bills. She didn't have the classic buxom look of a stripper, so she began turning tricks behind the club to bring up the wages. The boss fired her, but passed her number on to a cameraman; and the rest was history.

"I decided to call myself Magda Lynn," she said. "Magda because it is my middle name — Anna Magda. And Lynn because of the whole porn connection."

I looked at her blankly. As I said, not my specialist area.

"You know," she said. "Amber Lynn, Porsche Lynn, Ginger Lynn, Amber Lynn Bach. It's almost like a badge of royalty in the business, that name. And it goes so well with Magda. Magda Lynn — sounds like Magdalene. The whole sexy fallen woman thing. I have fallen wonderfully."

My head was beginning to buzz. Too much information. I had to get this back on track. "Tell me about the film project," I suggested. Bad mistake. She told the story in minute detail, every last irrelevant detail. But it could be summarised easily: she was doing a travel documentary.

"I am walking the pilgrim path, a repentant Magdalene," she said, "the fallen woman seeking redemption. It's a clothed role, unusual for me. But I reckon I have the range. I just walk bits of the path, talk to the people I meet, do a bit of history and fine dining. People watch travel programmes, you know." She said this as if it surprised her.

"I am sure it will be great," I said. "And the Church came on board and co-operated?" I knew that from the cardinal.

She scowled. "They said they would come on board, but I don't know how serious they are about the whole thing. They are letting us into the churches and stuff, but they aren't allowing us to film in there."

This was not what the cardinal had implied. He had implied an access-all-areas scenario, to draw out the killer. I might have to have a word with him.

"What restrictions are they putting on you?" I asked.

A look of anger crossed her pretty features. "I had a great idea for the final show of the series. It will be a four-parter, and when we get to Santiago, I wanted to shoot a scene in the cathedral. I thought it would be a great ending if I could do the parish priest at the end of the show. It kinda all leads up to that naturally."

My eyebrows didn't just rise, they almost levitated.

"Can you believe this? They won't allow me do the priest. They said that priests aren't allowed do chicks. No wonder they are all so fucking frustrated."

I nodded sympathetically. "You know Catholic priests are celibate?" I said.

"Of course I know. I am a Catholic myself," she said.

"Do you know what celibate means?"

"Yes. It means they can't marry. I never suspected it banned them from doing chicks. They won't even let me blow him."

"If they aren't allowed to marry, who did you think they were doing?"

"Nuns?" she said lamely.

It was going to be a long walk.

SEVEN

I was on my second beer. I normally don't do liquid lunches, but my meeting with Magda had disheartened me. Don't get me wrong; she was a lovely woman. But I didn't think she would be able to help me protect her. If there really was a killer on the loose, if he really would fall into the trap, it was going to be a difficult few weeks.

Of course, he might just ignore the trap. In which case, I was being well paid to take a holiday I didn't want. On balance, I thought I could live with that.

My phone binged. My brother. Damn. Like Magda, a nice guy. Unlike Magda, a pain in the ass. There were always problems. Generally with our sister, and generally I had to sort them out. Often while people were shooting at me.

With a theatrical sigh — although I was alone — I opened the text, and read.

Thinking of Mount Toubkal, then a few days on the beach with Serena. Can you organise it?

Mount Toubkal, in Morocco, is the highest peak in the Atlas Mountains, and the highest peak in the entire Arab world. At a tad over 4,000 metres, it is not technically difficult, but it presented difficulties of a whole different kind. The first was that being an adventure tour guide is just my cover; I don't actually do it. But I could get over that with a few phone calls. The real difficulty was that Lester is married to a woman called Chloe, and no matter how contrary your predictive text is, spell check does not change that to Serena. I would have to contact our sister Jane and find out what the hell was happening. After another beer.

Just then a shadow crossed my table, and a small, dapper man in a very neatly pressed police uniform appeared at my side. He had dark hair, heavily greased and teased into a pompadour, and a thin pencil moustache. Despite the heat, there was not the slightest hint of sweat on his pristine shirt. Just sitting in his presence made me feel like a slob.

"Senor Eliot?" he asked with a smile, as he pulled out a chair and sat across from me. He offered a hand, and his grip was surprisingly firm. "Inspector Victor Rodriguez. May I sit?"

He had already done so, so it seemed churlish to refuse him. And I had no outstanding parking or speeding tickets, so I wasn't worried.

"Paul Vandy," I said, as I pumped his hand.

"Yes. His Eminence told me that," he said.

Why I was bothering with the alias?

"We need to talk about what you are doing here. You understand, I am an officer of the law. I do not approve of any plan to assassinate our killer. It goes against everything I believe in. We capture killers, we don't kill them."

I nodded. That was my plan too. "I am not going to kill anyone. I have been hired as a bodyguard for Magda Lynn. Nothing more. I don't know where this idea that I am some killer for hire came from."

He nodded sagely, then went on: "After you kill him, there will be a lot of confusion. My men will be investigating the crime scene and looking for eye witnesses. There will be twelve, twenty-four hours of confusion, during which we will not know what is happening, and we will make no arrests. That is all I can give you. Will you need someone to drive you across the border, or have you that organised?"

"I am not going to kill anyone," I repeated.

"Message received and understood," he said, nodding. "So, you have made the getaway arrangements already. Good. Better I do not know them."

"I am not going to kill anyone," I said again.

"Good. We understand one another." He stretched his hand across and shook mine once more. "So, my colleagues and I will give you all co-operation in your efforts to not kill this man. Unless, of course, we catch him first." He smiled.

I smiled back, through gritted teeth. "That is the plan," I muttered.

He waved his hand vaguely in the air, and a small espresso appeared, alongside a shot of something that could have been Sambuca, or vodka, or a clear gin. I couldn't tell. He looked at me and I shook my head in negation. He waved his hand again, and the same two drinks appeared in front of me. I was wrong. It was a weird herbal liquor I had never tried before. He lifted his glass, and we clinked.

"Now to plans," he said. "We spring the trap tonight."

He could have slapped me in the face with a wet fish and he wouldn't have got a more surprised reaction. I thought there would be some planning, some logistics that I might be involved in.

"Is a simple plan," he said, his polished English slipping a little as he got excited. "We have organised a big press event, and a meet and greet with Señorita Magda after that. She will be left unprotected, and the killer will pounce. And presto, we put the finger up him."

"On him."

"On him, as you say. Do you kill him then?"

"I don't kill him at all. You put him on trial."

The officer's eyes lit up. "That would be my feather in the cap. If you do this for me, my men will drive you to the border, and see you across. No need for an elaborate getaway."

I knocked back the rest of the liquor. It didn't help. "One more thing," I said. "I was attacked as I came over the Napoleon Pass."

"Yes?" said Rodriguez. He looked like a man waiting for a punchline.

"Is it usual?"

He shrugged expressively. I could take it as a yes, a no, a token of sympathy, or a dismissal. Anything except a definite answer. I just looked at him, waiting. Eventually he said: "Not unusual, I suppose. People get mugged all the time."

"On the Camino? On a forest path?"

He shrugged again. "Perhaps a little unusual. But you were carrying a suitcase. That too is unusual. Everyone is talking about the mad Englishman and his suitcase."

"Scottish man. And a bit of a coincidence, being attacked when I came here to do a job."

Just then, Cardinal Benoluchi walked up and sat down at our small table. He made the same mason-like secret signal with a minimal wave of his hand, and a glass of wine appeared.

He looked at me, but I shook my head. I would have loved another drink, but it would not be wise. Not while I was working. I did wonder, though, if I waved my hands vaguely, would what I wanted be brought to the table? Perhaps a taxi to the airport and a ticket home?

"Victor, you have met Eliot?" said the cardinal.

"Paul," I corrected.

"We have reached an understanding. Tonight he will not kill our killer, and I will drive him to the border," the inspector

43

replied. A plan seemed to have been agreed, despite my best efforts.

I sighed. "Tell me how this goes down."

EIGHT

At three-thirty, I briefed Fermin Benoluchi and Victor Rodriguez.

"The plan is bonkers," I opened. "We can't spring a trap if we are not ready."

"But we are ready," said Rodriguez. "I am here, you are here. Magda is here. What more do we need?"

"Oh, I don't know. Perhaps a gun for me? In my line of work, I often find those useful."

Cardinal Benoluchi looked glum. "I assumed you would come with what you needed."

"I flew commercial."

"And you don't have…?"

"No, I don't have a special briefcase with lead lining that allows me to bring my guns through security. I assumed I would have a day or two to prepare. There are ways, but not if you are in a hurry."

Rodriguez smiled. "I can help."

He reached into his jacket and took out an undersized pistol. He slid it across the table. He didn't even glance up to see whether anyone was watching. I quickly covered the piece with a napkin and looked at it surreptitiously. It was a discontinued model, a SIG Sauer Mosquito. About 10% smaller than a regular SIG, and fired .22s. The thing about a .22 is, it will kill — but you have to be lucky, or an amazing shot. Hit an artery and your victim will bleed out. Hit him right between the eyes and he goes down like a sack of potatoes. But hit a big man in the gut, he mightn't even register he's been shot. It is a pea shooter.

"That's it?"

"It's my throw-down weapon," he shrugged.

Throw-down weapon — the spare gun some cops keep on hand in case they get involved in a shooting incident and need to claim the other guy, who was unarmed, shot first. They just throw down the spare gun after firing off a random round for the forensics, and walk away. The throw-down is often cheap, and rarely well maintained. Great. Just what I needed.

"It's only got a ten-shot mag," I pointed out. "Do you have a spare clip?"

"Just what's in it," he said sadly.

I picked up the gun and released the magazine. It felt light. Six shots. That was my weapon. Could the day get worse?

At four, I briefed Magda. She wasn't wearing a protective vest, because I didn't think the killer would try a shot. Didn't seem his style. The inspector agreed. Magda threw in her cent's worth: a vest would hide her decolletage, so it wouldn't be happening.

I didn't argue the point, because we didn't actually have a vest.

Her instructions were to stick close to me, and to cling to me like a limpet if things got hairy, or if too many fans showed up. Personally, I thought it was unlikely we would get any fans. I had never heard of her before yesterday, and I doubted she was a big draw in rural Spain. But my co-conspirators were sure the evening event would be a sell-out.

"And afterwards?" asked Magda, a twinkle in her eye. "Do we play our Whitney and Costner game? You must come to my bed." She ran a finger seductively down my face, and I think I blushed.

The cardinal laughed. "Leave the man alone, Miss Lynn," he said. "He is not a Catholic, so I can't forgive him afterwards."

The press conference was held, bizarrely, in a graveyard beside an old church within the walled medieval section of Pamplona. The cardinal and Magda sat on loungers among the tombstones, side by side, while the inspector and I mingled with the crowd. Rodriguez was in plain clothes, but to my mind he looked a bit too neat for the job. The crease on his trousers could have cut cheese. He looked as casual as a tux in a strip club. One look told you he was being paid to be here, and he was the security. I have to admit I did manage to pull off the pilgrim look. I had spent the afternoon on a shopping spree, and had managed to get a pair of boots, cut-off jeans, and a few generic T-shirts. I stuffed the clothes I wasn't wearing into a rucksack, and left an old towel hanging out of it. The suitcase went in a bin. I would pass inspection.

I stayed away from Rodriguez. I lounged, scanning the crowd. Nothing suspicious. No one who looked like they didn't belong. But that's the thing with psychopaths. They blend. You can live beside one for years without ever suspecting his mind and morals are out of kilter. Easier by far to spot a paid assassin like me. We have a look. Hard, alert. Even in repose the pros look like a coiled spring. But I wasn't looking for a pro, and no one was standing out. My hinky radar was not pinging.

Out of the corner of my eye, I thought I saw something familiar. I turned, but there was nothing. Just a rucksack disappearing into a hostel. I dismissed it, but kept half an eye on the hostel for the next twenty minutes. Nothing.

The press conference was more of a photo opportunity. Magda posed in front of the main door to the chapel beside the graveyard. She sprawled seductively on a grave, until someone whispered to her that it might not be appropriate. She used a cross as a pole and gave us some moves, until the same voice whispered that it might not be appropriate. She scowled, but did it prettily. Then, pictures snapped, she answered questions from the press. Just two reporters had shown up, both from local rags. The questions were mundane. How was the walk? How did she find the local food? Were the local señors attractive?

It was almost over when I spotted her.

She was coming out of the hostel; I had been keeping half an eye on an attractive woman with dark hair. As soon as I turned, I knew what had caught my gaze earlier. It was Liz, the woman who had sent me down the wrong path to my muggers.

She turned and began to walk towards the historic quarter. Could I follow her? My job was to protect the target, but the target was safe. She was surrounded by the photographer and the two journalists, their tongues hanging out like dogs panting. Inspector Rodriguez was not far away, scanning the crowd. The cardinal was at a discreet distance. He did not want to appear too eager. A picture of him beside a pole dancing porno actress gyrating around a crucifix would not have gone down well with the Curia in Rome. But he was close enough to enjoy the performance, and I could see the grin on his face. He really was not living up to my expectations of a Catholic cleric.

Could I follow her?

My dilemma was solved when Liz turned and spotted me. She looked slightly puzzled for a moment, then her face lit up with a strong smile, and she changed direction. She was heading straight towards me.

I smiled.

Play it cool.

"Paul!" she grinned. "I almost didn't recognise you. You've gone pilgrim." She looked at my clothes appreciatively.

"Felt I had to blend in," I said. "Once I was here, I decided to do it properly. I've bought a rucksack and ditched the suitcase. Sent it home to Scotland. How have you been getting on?"

"Oh, you know. Long days. Tired feet. Blisters. The descent into Zubiri was no fun. But I got there very early, so I walked on to here. The people I meet are so nice. So on balance, all good."

I nodded. "Yesterday, you told me about a shortcut?"

"Did I? Oh yes, the turn to the left."

I nodded and lost the grin. "That turn led me off the path and into the forest. Where I was mugged."

She looked shocked for a moment, then recovered. "Impossible," she said. "I took that turn myself. It led straight down to the monastery. Through the trees. Took a mile off the official path."

It was my turn to look confused. The turn was nowhere near the monastery. "It was ten kilometres earlier than that, before we even reached the top of the Napoleon Pass," I said.

She smiled, but without warmth. "You are mistaken," she said. "I told you about the turn before the top of the pass. But the turn itself was on the other side of the pass, on the descent to Roncesvalles."

I looked at her. I thought it out. There had been a turn a few miles above the forested monastery. The obvious path wound down the hill in a series of S loops, to disappear into the belt of trees at the bottom. The other path was a rough ribbon through the ragged bushes and on into an elm forest. Most people took the path, but a few hardy souls plunged into the trees and followed the steep and stony path down. Hard on the knees, but it would have shortened my journey had I followed them.

Now it was my turn to look confused. Had this all been an honest mistake? Or was I right in suspecting Liz had set me up to be attacked? Both suddenly seemed equally plausible.

"See you around, Paul," she said, and was gone. I now had more questions than ever.

NINE

We had a coffee. It had been a bit of a flop. No one had attacked Magda. No one had been flushed out.

"You never got the chance to kill him," muttered Rodriguez sympathetically.

That was the only good thing to come from the press event.

Magda was upbeat. She knew, or suspected, she was being used in some way by the Church, but she also knew it was giving her access to places she could not have got to without their co-operation. And I don't really believe that she took her security seriously. It was all a game to her.

"All you men are so glum," she said. "Enjoy."

She was drinking wine while we had coffees, so I could see how she was enjoying it. But the rest of us were working. Even the cardinal.

"We'll try again tomorrow," he said glumly. "There is the photo op on top of the ridge."

The photo op — I was not happy with that. Not one little bit. The idea was that the following day we would take a taxi out of Pamplona and drive to a village about twenty kilometres away. Then we would be on foot. We would walk to a high ridge that marks the high point of that portion of the Camino, then spread out a picnic lunch and let people come over and have their picture taken with Magda. The inspector was sure it would work. The cardinal less so. I was very sceptical. If I didn't know who she was, did she really have a fan base? But what did I know?

At least we were staying in a good hotel that night, not one of the grotty pilgrim hostels. We went back and I showered. When I came down to the lobby, the inspector was missing. He was on duty, and his *per diem* allowance did not cover hotels. He was in a guest house on the outskirts of the city. He would join us at the restaurant. I had a feeling Victor was not one to forego free dinners. The cardinal was missing, too. He was in the bridal suite, alone, having a snooze. The Catholic Church provides its princes with a better *per diem* than the Spanish police, obviously. Magda was missing — upstairs doing the mysterious things glamorous women do to keep themselves glamorous, I supposed. So I ordered a Cardhu and relaxed.

The Cardhu, a lowland malt whisky, came with ice. So I sent it back. How could a professional waiter have done that?

The drink came back naked, the way the gods of whisky intended. I dipped a spoon into the jug of water it came with, then stirred the wet spoon through the measure of scotch. Apparently it opens out the flavours, without diluting them. What do I know? I sipped. Smooth and mild. Not my normal choice, but pleasant enough. Automatically I scanned the room. I couldn't switch off. No one pinged my spidey senses. Then a tall, slim man in his early forties walked in, and the hairs on the back of my neck stood to attention.

TEN

I looked at him carefully. There was nothing about him that stood out. He appeared depressingly normal. Thinning hair, glasses, a black shirt that hugged his thin chest, and round glasses that are apparently trendy. His shoulders were slightly stooped and he carried himself with a slight air of diffidence. All together, someone who would disappear into the background. So why were the hairs on my neck tingling?

I ran through a mugshot book in my head. A useless exercise, because he would not be in it. But then I got a hit. He was a dead ringer for John Christie, the London serial killer in the post war years who managed to pass the blame onto a neighbour, Timothy Evans. Evans got a suspended sentence — the sort that involved a long drop and a broken neck. This miscarriage of justice was one of the reasons the death penalty was abolished in the UK.

Christie had eventually been caught. Even if he hadn't, he would be 119 now. So this clearly was not him. As suspected, the mugshot book in my head had drawn a blank. But maybe I now knew why he was bugging me. So I dismissed the stranger from my thoughts and focused all my attention on the malt.

A few minutes later, Magda appeared. No, she made an entrance. I have often heard that said of beautiful women and charismatic actresses. They make an entrance. But for the first time I understood the expression. Magda owned the room.

She was wearing a short black dress that exposed a lot of flesh, but somehow managed to make that look classy. I won't even try to describe what she was wearing. Fashionistas know those secrets, but they are beyond the ken of the ordinary man.

All I will say is that I was under her spell, just like every other man in the room.

Every other man bar Mr Christie. John Christie barely glanced up at her. I revised my assessment. Not a creepy accountant on an evening off. Creepy gay accountant on an evening off.

Magda smiled at me, and bent down to kiss me on the cheek. Her smile deserved a wattage rating of its own. Her cleavage deserved a wattage rating too. She sat beside me and a waiter was over in seconds. She smiled at him and he disappeared, arriving back a moment later with a flute of champagne.

"How do you do that?" I asked.

She just smiled enigmatically. I could get tired of that smile. Actually, no, I couldn't.

"Do you know him?" I asked quietly, looking in the direction of the accountant.

She followed my gaze, and her face creased in disgust, before resuming its habitual smile. "Never seen him before," she lied.

"Really?" I held her gaze.

She held my gaze for a moment, then turned away. "I know his type," she said. "A conservative, probably a Christian, who condemns my lifestyle but secretly watches my scenes on his own with one hand in his lap. He sees me now in the flesh and he is disgusted — but he probably has a boner in his pants."

I shrugged. Could be. There was probably just something in his face or his body language that triggered an atavistic reaction in us. I dismissed him from my thoughts.

The cardinal walked in and joined us. He was dressed in his civvies — grey slacks, white shirt, and a natty tweed sport coat. I noticed his silk tie was a deep purple.

He caught me looking. "I like to sport the colours even when I am enjoying a rare night off," he said. "If I wore the dog collar and chaperoned a beautiful woman, it would start the tongues to wag."

"You look sharp, Fermin. We almost have a full house," I said. "Is Inspector Rodriguez joining us?"

"Victor will join us at the restaurant. He is staying in a different hotel."

Around seven, we strolled out. The streets were full of life and noise. Weary pilgrims rubbed shoulders with young Americans following the footsteps of Papa Hemingway and local youths promenading. It was a scene of life and bustle common to all Latin cultures, and I enjoyed it, despite one side of my brain remaining on high alert. I was here to work, not to show off to the ladies.

Pamplona is the start of pinchos country. Throughout Spain, the little bar snacks you feast on are known as tapas. But in the northern regions they become pinchos, and they are a gourmet's delight. Everywhere we passed, people were at small tables outside bars eating delicate morsels of food. My mouth was watering.

"Patience," smiled Fermin. "We have a reservation at one of the best places."

His idea of a reservation turned out to be a little different from mine. He meant we had agreed to meet there at seven-thirty. He had not passed that information on to the staff at the bar, and there was no table for us. We crowded at the bar and elbowed some space for ourselves.

It was not so bad for Magda. She swanned in and a path cleared before her, as men gallantly gave up their space. But when I tried to follow in her wake the space miraculously closed, and I was left trying to force my way through a rugby scrum. But eventually we found ourselves on three stools by the bar, Magda holding court on the centre one.

I ordered a slice of fried foie gras, a small plate of salted cod in tomato sauce, a side of patatas bravas, a delicious mushroom open sandwich, and a small blood pudding. The five plates appeared on the counter before me, with five small glasses of red wine.

I looked at the barman. "I didn't order wine," I said.

"Pardon," he muttered, and began to replace the five glasses with five small beers.

"I didn't order beer either," I protested.

He shrugged. "Beer or wine, I don't mind. But you must have one."

"I just want the food."

"Food comes with the drink."

"But you don't have to give me the drink if I don't want to drink," I pointed out.

He shrugged. "It's done now," he said. And that was the last word on the matter.

Magda was grinning like a Cheshire cat. "Down them all, I dare you. I'd love to see you drunk."

All fun and games until the killer strikes, I thought. But grimly I lifted one of the beers — there were two beers and three red wines in front of me by that point.

The cardinal, fair play, came to my rescue, by taking the three wines and pouring them into one large glass. "Altar wine has built up my immunity," he explained. "I can drink this babies' milk by the litre."

A few minutes later, Inspector Rodriguez elbowed his way to the bar. I watched his progress. People seemed to instinctively move out of his way. It was as if they smelt cop off him. Very quickly he was sitting beside the cardinal, and the chair opposite him was empty. We had breathing space.

He reached across and took the spare beer.

"Help yourself, why don't you, Victor?" I said.

He nodded. "I will take some to help you out, as you are on duty."

"And you are not?"

"I know the criminal mind. All is good for this evening. When the press conference didn't flush him out, we are safe until the photo opportunity and the meet-and-greet tomorrow."

I was less sure. But Magda was surrounded by a seasoned cop and an alert hitman. I thought she should be safe. Visually she was cordoned by three men. That might have been enough to put off anyone with trouble on his mind. And two of the men were trained to handle themselves when the bullets began to fly. I decided to relax and enjoy the evening.

I did. I love good food. And it was good. Very good. I got used to the weird ordering system. I would point to what I wanted. The plate would appear before me a few minutes later with a small glass of red wine. I would eat the food and ignore the wine, and a few minutes later the glass would mysteriously disappear. I noticed the cardinal's eyes appeared to be glassing over slightly. I am sure the two were related.

Around nine we decided to move to a proper restaurant. We got up and let Magda lead the way. I was right behind her. As she left the bar and walked onto the street, all my senses were on alert. This was the crucial moment, but I was close enough to her that nothing could happen.

Then something did happen.

There was a sudden movement to Magda's left and a shadow passed between me and the door, temporarily blocking my view. I reacted instinctively, leaping forward and pushing past a loved-up couple trying to enter the bar. The man gesticulated angrily, but I ignored him. I was outside, frantically searching for the threat, and for Magda.

She was behind me. She looked startled. So did the large nun who had rudely pushed past her and blocked my view for a moment.

"Young man," she muttered frostily, "show some manners."

ELEVEN

We ended up in a restaurant with its own Michelin star. A rare treat for me, but common enough in this part of Spain. The region around San Sebastian — and we were only a few hours' drive from there — has the highest concentration of Michelin star restaurants on the planet.

"My treat," smiled the cardinal, confirming my suspicion that the Church has far too much money for an organisation that believes rich men can squeeze through the eye of a needle easier than entering the gates of Heaven. I know the Eye of the Needle was one of the gates of ancient Jerusalem, but still, if I judged the cardinal on his precepts, he was going to the hot place. Luckily I am an atheist, so I was just going to enjoy the meal on his dime.

Unfortunately, I had enjoyed too many pinchos in the first bar, and my stomach urged caution. So I ordered two starters and no entree.

"You know these swanky restaurants serve portions so small you'll want to stop by a McDonalds on the way home?" said Cardinal Benoluchi. "So push the boat out and go for the entree. Mother Church is paying. I can't forgive you if you fornicate with our delightful Magda, or if you kill our killer, but I can at least see you are well fed while you are in our employ."

I shrugged, and added a wild venison burrito in chocolate chilli sauce to my order. I would work it off in the morning on our walk to the photo op. The honey trap.

Magda ordered a salad, which distressed the cardinal.

"Please, just eat," he tried to insist.

"I have to watch my figure," she replied.

"You get the steak, I can watch your figure for the evening," he said. There was a distinctly non-clerical gleam in his eye. He caught my stare. "Being celibate is like being on a diet. I can still look at the menu."

The meal was delicious. My starters were divine. Magda's salad was rich and calorie laden. But the portions, true to Benoluchi's assessment, were small. I had plenty of room for my burrito.

It was minute but perfectly formed. I was just applying the business edge of my knife to it when the hairs on the back of my head stood to attention. It was like they were on parade and the sergeant major had just walked into the square and snapped his crop. My neck actually tingled. I noticed Magda tense.

Inspector Rodriguez was too busy with his sixth glass of wine to notice. His copper's nose had deserted him about four glasses ago.

Without appearing to move, I slowly straightened in my chair and my eyes began to rove the room. I looked at Magda, and she was looking over my left shoulder, towards the entrance. Her eyes moved to the left, following something or someone. So I dropped a napkin, and leaned down to pick it up. That gave me a perfect view.

John Christie had just walked into the restaurant. As I watched, he muttered softly to the maître d', then moved to a table by the wall to the right of the entrance. The table was a small one, and he sat with his back to the wall. As I straightened, I could see he was sitting with a direct line of sight to Magda, his gaze burning into the back of my head.

Betraying no movement with my head, I hissed across the table at her. She didn't even seem to notice. So I kicked her ankle under the table. She jumped slightly and turned to me.

"You told me you didn't know him," I said. "You lied. Spill."

She scowled. "He is my stalker. All beautiful women have stalkers."

"I need more."

"What more is there? He has been following me, stalking me if you will, for eighteen months. We have a restraining order against him in Germany. He can't come within 200 metres of me. But out here, that obviously doesn't apply. I suppose he heard the publicity about me being here, and he's taking his chance." She smiled slightly, as if she admired his persistence.

"And you never thought to tell me any of this?"

"Georg is harmless. He has never touched me. He's an over-eager fan, nothing more. He is not a danger."

"Let me be the judge of that."

But as we progressed through our courses, and the little amuse-bouches the waiter brought between them, I began to relax. Georg seemed to be harmless. He was eating his own dinner, and would have passed inspection if it wasn't for the fact that he occasionally glared over at Magda.

At one point she stood to use the restroom. I began to stand.

"Oh please," she said, placing a warm hand on my chest. "I hardly need a chaperone."

The restroom was on the far side of the restaurant, and she did not need to pass Mr Christie — now Georg — to reach it. So I watched her cross the room, and kept him in my view with my peripheral vision. He barely reacted, grappling instead with his plate. I relaxed.

Then she came out of the restroom, and instead of coming back to our table, she deliberately crossed the floor, stopping by his small table. I was too far away to catch what she said, but she ran a finger seductively down his cheek and kissed the top of his head. Then she was back at our table, and Cardinal Benoluchi stood up to pull out her chair for her.

"What the hell are you up to?"

"His name is Georg Fleischmann, and he is completely harmless. I was just saying hello. If he behaves, I throw him the odd bone. See how he smiles?" She gave a small wave in his direction. I turned, and he was smiling back, wearing the look of a besotted teenager.

"That will keep him happy for a while. He's got his fix. He'll stop annoying me now. That is how it works."

And ignoring my look, she picked up her fork and went back to her dessert.

After our coffees, we stepped out into the warm night air. The streets were still crowded, but the crowd was thinning. We were approaching midnight, and all the pilgrims were in bed. The locals were still enjoying the nightlife, and the American tourists were feeling decadent simply by being up after ten. The vibe was mellow.

Benoluchi hailed a cab. "I will leave the walking to you young people. I am too old and too full of good food for that," he said, and was gone.

The inspector smiled. "I will walk you back to your hotel, then walk on to my own," he said. He didn't even glance back once. I did. I checked out the restaurant. Georg Fleischmann was still sitting at his table, staring vacantly at the seat that had been occupied by Magda. A waiter came along, and he started slightly, then looked up and smiled as his dessert was placed in front of him. He picked up his fork.

Magda was right. We had nothing to fear from this loser.

We began walking, back towards the historic quarter and the still-beating heart of the city. The sounds of laughter and music grew. Magda began to shimmy her hips, keeping time to the music pouring out of one of the busier bars. She stopped at the door and danced alone for a moment. It was graceful and alluring, and when she moved on, a table gently clapped her passing. She could own a street.

At the end of the street we turned down a lane. It was dark and none of the windows showed any light. A few bins were out, ready for the morning collection. A cat sniffed at one. I was on alert, but not full alert. I had eventually taken two glasses of wine and a digestif, and in tests that was enough alcohol to reduce my reaction time. In practice, my reaction time is so far off the charts that it would take a lot more than that to bring me down to regular levels. I was still capable of reacting instantly to a threat. There was no threat.

The small laneway turned left, into a longer dark street. At the end of that, we would turn right down one of the main streets of the town, and we were only a few minutes from our hotel. Night over; no assassination attempts.

Then a bin fell over, the metal lid clanking loudly in the street, it's peal echoing off the stone walls of the buildings.

I turned instantly, and a fist hit me square on the jaw, dropping me to the ground.

TWELVE

The ground was cobble stones, and I hit it hard with my back and shoulders. My head should have snapped back and bounced off the stones, probably knocking me out. But as I said, just three units of alcohol. I am too highly trained for that.

As I fell, I straightened in the air, and took the fall with my back and shoulders. More my back, but I rolled slightly at the last moment, taking enough on my shoulders not to wind me. And my arms whipped down, slapping the pavement. The energy of the fall was dissipated without my feeling too much pain. And my head was tucked firmly into my chin. That is the first rule when you fall backwards; look at your belly button. It forces your chin down to your chest, and prevents your head whiplashing back into the pavement.

So when I got over the initial shock of the punch, I almost bounced back to my feet. Like one of those inflatable toy punchbags kids have, I was up before I fully processed the fact that I had been down.

But my attacker had stepped to the side, and I was facing the wrong way. Before I could turn, I felt a blow to my kidneys that took the wind out of me and dropped me to my knees. I was down for the second time, and I still hadn't even seen my attacker.

My hands hit the ground and I was on all-fours, crawl position, and about to throw up. But I swallowed it back, and focused on bringing the wave of pain under control. You can never block the pain, you just ride the wave. You accept it as a message from your nerves that something is wrong, and you go with it. That allows you to function, just about.

I crawled in a semicircle until I was facing back up the street. The inspector was sitting on the ground, rubbing a wound to his head that was beginning to bleed badly. He looked confused.

And on his feet was John Christie. No, Georg Fleischmann. In his hand gleamed an extendable baton. That was what had caught me in the kidneys. That was what had given the inspector the love bite on his forehead. Moonlight glinted on the weapon as he raised it high overhead, and directly in front of him I could see the terrified face of Magda.

If I had stood, I would have lost too much time. Instead, I stretched forward with my hand. It felt weak, but as it moved I rode the wave and accepted the pain, and the strength came back. I grasped his trouser leg firmly, then jerked it back towards me.

With a howl of surprise, his foot left the ground and he crashed down on one knee, the blow he had just started sailing harmlessly in front of Magda.

I came forward another half foot and clamped my teeth firmly on his Achilles tendon, biting down and digging in.

He howled in fury and pain, twisting his body to attack me. But I had him now. Once I get a grip, I am tenacious. And unless you have been trained to fight on the ground, you can't punch or kick effectively. I had been trained. Fleischmann had not.

It was a mercifully short fight. Fleischmann twisted and swung ineffectually against me, his weak blow bouncing off my shoulder. But now he was in my personal space, and like a spider cocooning a fly, I reeled him in. Maintaining my grip on his trouser leg, I moved my other hand up and hooked his arm.

Then I released his leg as I used the leverage of his arm to swing him onto his back, and I swung onto his chest. Two hammer fists to his face and he stopped moving. Ground and pound, baby.

I stood up and helped the inspector to his feet.

"Good work, my friend. I would have stood up and done it myself, but you seemed to have it well under control." He reached into his suit pocket and removed a bag of industrial strength cable ties.

"No cuffs?" I joked.

"Cuffs are so eighties. He won't move with these on."

I watched as cable ties went on ankles and wrists, then the inspector pulled Fleischmann to the side of the alley, sitting him up against a wall. He was beginning to come around. So was the inspector, I thought.

I looked at Magda and was about to say something when her face dissolved into a mask of tears. Then she fell into my arms.

THIRTEEN

There were just two of us on the street. The inspector had called for a car, and had remained with his prisoner. We had walked on.

"He was never dangerous before," said Magda, for the twentieth time.

"You can never tell what will trigger an episode," I said. Also for the twentieth time. "And you need a drink."

This was said for the first time. It had suddenly struck me that a twenty-minute sojourn in one of the bars would return her to an even keel. I needed her calm. It is far easier to protect someone who is calm and behaving predictably.

Twenty minutes later we were back on the street, and she *was* calmer. Aside from a certain frantic gleam in her eye, she seemed to be herself again. Two glasses of wine — and a coffee for me — had restored the natural order.

"I want to walk for a while. I am too keyed up to go back to the hotel."

We walked aimlessly for a few minutes, as the streets emptied of revellers. We had left the old quarter and were in a more residential area. Ahead of us was a big round structure that looked like a football stadium.

Magda's eyes suddenly lit up. "It's the bullring," she said.

She was right — up ahead of us was the ring that the bulls charge into after the famous run through the streets of Pamplona, the ring made famous by Papa Hemingway.

"Wrong day," she sighed. "We could have run with the bulls. That must be some buzz." She smiled at me. "Have you done it?"

"No," I lied.

Just then something small and wet struck me on the cheek, and I looked up. Magda looked up. And the heavens opened. A sudden rainstorm sprayed down, instantly drenching us. The drops were as big as thimbles, falling straight and true like a power shower. I tried to get my arms over my head, but it was no use. The water quickly penetrated to my skin, rendering my thin shirt useless. Magda straightened up and held her arms out, like a sacrifice. She was smiling. Her black number clung to her body, and I suddenly wished she had been wearing a white blouse. Juvenile, I know.

"Let's do our own bull run. Race you to the bus shelter," she said.

And she was off, her laughter tinkling in the night air. Laughing myself, I followed her. She had a few yards on me, and her stride was long. I could have lengthened mine, or upped the cadence, but I liked the view so I stayed a step behind. I would swoop past at the last moment.

She tried to stop as she drew close to the bus shelter, but as she turned the strap of her leather shoe snapped, and the shoe came off. She was suddenly sliding on the wet paving stones. Her legs slid to the ground first, almost gracefully, and the rest of her body slid into place behind them. She came to a halt on her back, looking up at the dark clouds, her face shiny and luminous from the water. I bent down to pick her up, but she pulled me down and our lips met. Her lips were soft and plump, and tasted of cherry. Then her tongue found its way into my mouth, and mine found its way into hers. It was a delicious kiss, long and lingering. There was real passion in it, real promise.

But then I pulled back. "I'm sorry," I said. "I was hurt in my last relationship. I am not ready for this."

"This might be just a one night thing — you are ready for a one night thing."

I shook my head sadly. But she was still clinging to me. Her hand rubbed down my chest, rubbed down past my belt, brushed my groin, and I felt myself stiffen.

"You are ready," she said.

"Not in my head," I said reluctantly, standing up and pulling her to her feet.

We walked on in silence for a few minutes. There was still something between us.

"They say that the best sex you will ever have is with a woman you love," she said.

"I have heard that," I agreed.

"It's complete bullshit. The best sex you will ever have is with a professional. We do this for a living. We know what buttons to push, we know where to touch, and how hard. I could play you like a virtuoso plays a violin. It would be the greatest night of your life."

A part of me knew she was right, and I felt a tinge of regret.

FOURTEEN

The next morning, we all suffered from various degrees of big head syndrome. I was first down to breakfast, and I had a big head because I had saved the life of a porn queen, and got kissed by the same porn queen. Big boy fantasy become reality, and it felt good even if I knew it was going no further.

Next to appear was Benoluchi, who had a big head because he forgot you don't mix the grape and the grain. Many sips of the altar wine over a lifetime had not inured him to the amount of alcohol he had consumed the previous evening. He had mixed the grain and the grape, and a whole lot more besides.

"I don't have a hangover," he said irritably. "I am just frustrated."

I raised an eyebrow. It was my Roger Moore impression. I was feeling sophisticated.

He scowled. "Yes, frustrated. I am still a young man."

He was pushing sixty, and from the wrong side. But I let it slide.

"I look at a lady like Magda, and I think I should have been a Lutheran. This celibacy is a curse."

I could see he was serious, and I felt for him. "Have you ever…?"

He gave me a wink. "A gentleman never tells." Then he smiled sadly, and went on: "Never. I fell in love in the seminary forty years ago, but it never went beyond an innocent kiss. We are still good friends. She is happily married now. I look at my sister and she has two children. I believe I am a good uncle. I was never happier than when I was playing with those two boys. I often wonder what sort of a father I would have made. But it is too late now. Even if mother Church was to lift the ban on marriage, my time has passed. I am still a man, but not so young that the ladies even notice me anymore."

I didn't know how to respond, but just then a waiter dropped a plate, and the loud clang as it shattered caused the cardinal to wince.

"Please," he muttered, holding his head in his hands.

Magda was next to appear. I was surprised to see that for once she did not make an entrance. She just came into the dining room, looked around, spotted us and walked over. There was a distinct lack of bounce in her step, and she looked her age. I have no idea how old she was, but she was not walking like an eighteen-year-old this morning.

Benoluchi made an effort to be his usual gallant self. He stood and shuffled out her chair for her. Magda sat heavily.

"Rough night?"

She nodded at him. "My stalker followed us from the restaurant," she said. "He attacked Eliot and the inspector, but luckily Eliot was able to handle him." She smiled at me, and it looked like death warmed up.

Cardinal Benoluchi blanched slightly. "Were you hurt?"

"No, but the inspector took a bit of a beating."

I had taken a bit of a beating too, but I didn't remind anyone. I am a big boy, and I get over these things. My jaw felt fine this morning. Do enough rounds of sparring and you get that way. There was a vicious bruise over my abdomen where the baton had caught me, but that would heal in a few days. It wouldn't stop me doing anything aside from stomach crunches, and I don't crunch.

"Where is he now?" asked the cardinal.

"The inspector?"

"No — your stalker. I hope he is not still out there looking for you."

I shook my head. "The inspector took him into custody. One less thing for us to worry about."

Just then the waiter arrived with a steaming jug of coffee. The Spanish do their coffee well, and the cardinal brightened visibly when he smelt the pungent aroma. He poured a small cup and sipped it appreciatively, then knocked it back. Then he remembered his manners, and poured one for Magda.

There was silence until they were on their second cups, and I was savouring my first. The cardinal sighed deeply, and Magda echoed him.

"Don't look so smug," she said to me in mock severity. "You won't always be on duty. When this is over, I will get you so drunk you won't know your arse from your … oh, forget it. Just pour me another coffee."

It was at that point that the inspector arrived. He looked as dapper as ever. He must have brought a whole suitcase full of fresh shirts. But his eyes were bloodshot, and his face was ashen. He sat down. There was no cup for him, so he emptied the sugar cubes out of the bowl onto a small plate, and filled the sugar bowl with coffee. He lifted it with two hands and sipped gratefully. He put down the bowl, looked around at us, and risked a smile.

"All good?" I asked.

He nodded.

"After the incident last night?"

He nodded again. "My people, they came along."

"Good," I said. "And Fleischmann is in custody?"

He took another sip from the sugar bowl.

"Fleischmann is in custody?" I repeated.

"My people are dealing with the Fleischmann situation. I am an inspector. That is beneath my pay grade. I order, they execute."

"So he is in custody?"

"Too much talk for so early in the morning. Let us get breakfast and talk after that."

Something stunk. I reached across and snapped the bowl from his hands. Benoluchi looked shocked. Even Magda registered a mild look of surprise.

"Inspector, what are you not telling us?" I glared at him.

He met my glare, then looked away. "I was bringing him in. He was in the back seat, I was driving. But his hands were cuffed in front of his body, not behind. And he got his hands around my neck and he choked me. The car went out of control and we crashed."

"Was there not someone else in the car with you?" asked Magda.

"I was alone with him."

"What about your pay grade?" I asked sarcastically.

"Fuck the pay grade. It was my arrest."

The cardinal and I stared at one another. Magda had gone pale, some achievement considering how pasty she had looked all morning.

"He is now a fugitive. My people will find him," said the inspector defiantly.

"So that means…?"

The cardinal finished my thought. "He's out there, and he's not playing nice anymore."

FIFTEEN

It was after ten when we got moving. There was still no word from the inspector's people. Fleischmann was loose, and he could have been any place. Cable ties make great handcuffs, but you don't need to find a blacksmith or a locksmith to take them off. A kitchen knife or a piece of broken glass would suffice. So he was free and unencumbered. I didn't believe he was our serial killer, but he was a distraction I didn't need. Personal security is not my area, and for my first job I was getting attacked potentially on two fronts. And I knew now the value of the inspector as back-up.

So it was a sombre party that set out from Pamplona. We took a taxi, followed by the film crew's Land Cruiser, out to the next stop on the Camino, the little village of Cizur Minor. The crew was minimal: just two people. One was the cameraman, who also handled sound. His name was Mack and he sounded Australian. He seemed to look down his nose at the work he was doing, but he knew it paid his bills. The other crew member was Amanda, a slightly uptight English woman. She was nominally the director; but she also held the second camera when needed, and acted (reluctantly) as Magda's PA. Luckily, Magda wasn't a diva.

The ride took about half an hour, and we got out at the edge of the village. Magda was dressed in denim hot-pants and a tight white T-shirt tied up at the navel. She was showing more leg than a Russian long jumper. I helped her with her rucksack. It was enormous, yet it weighed under two kilos.

"Styrofoam," she laughed. "My real luggage travels in the crew car."

"A lot of walkers bring water for the journey," I pointed out.

"Who drinks water? Fish fuck in it."

With that she turned and flounced down the dusty trail that led from the village. She wiggled seductively as she passed the camera, then struck off with long strides. Within minutes she had caught up with a group of four walkers, and she fell into easy conversation with them. The cameraman dutifully followed, huffing to keep up. I hung back. Not only was the view good — Magda's shorts were tight — but it was my job to hang back.

The trail led across a patch of level ground, green and verdant, for about a kilometre. Then we came to a belt of trees, and once we cleared the trees the ground became a lot more dusty. Vegetation became sparser and the trail began to rise gently. It led obliquely towards a ridge of hills, many surmounted by windmills. I noticed that Magda began to fall behind the group of walkers. They didn't wait for her. It's the way of the Camino. You are on a personal journey, and if you don't keep up your companions will reconfigure their personal journey without your company. You find your own pace and stick to it for the day.

Other groups of walkers began to drift up to her, then past her. Her stride shortened. The sexy sway of her hips changed. I lengthened my stride slightly and easily closed the distance between us.

"Buen Camino," I said, the standard greeting on the way.

"And fuck you too," she replied.

"Going that well?"

"I thought I was fit. I can do two hour scenes with all sorts of awkward positions, yet this is killing me. Does this road ever slope down?"

"You don't even want to know about down," I told her. "That's when it gets seriously gnarly. Uphill is the easy bit. Why don't you stop and have some water? Oh yes, Styrofoam."

She glared as I laughed. I passed over my water bottle, and she sipped gratefully.

"It's lacking whisky," she said, as she passed it back.

We walked on, I in companionable silence, she in misery. The road continued for about two kilometres, and she did find her rhythm. Slowing down slightly was the trick. If you are not used to marching, march at a slow pace. The human body is a well-designed machine and capable of long distances with minimal fuss. After thirty minutes she was smiling again, and chatting amiably to me.

Then the path turned, and we were on the flank of the hill. The sun was out, blazing down on us. There wasn't even a breeze. And there was no shelter.

The constant repetitions of "Buen Camino" as walkers passed us began to grate. I could have put her on my back and jogged up the hill, but that was hardly the point. It was about Magda's pilgrimage. This was the moment of suffering that would sell the documentary, and Mack the cameraman, who was following us, was loving it. I admired his dedication. He would charge up ahead of us, set up his camera, take the shot, then run on ahead again. Sometimes he stayed behind and deployed a drone, getting dramatic aerial shots of both Magda and the terrain. But then he had to do some serious running to catch up with us. He was like the Energizer Bunny on acid. I stayed carefully out of these shots, rejoining Magda only when he moved on again.

It was a tough hour. We reached the small village of Zariquiegui, where I refilled my water bottles. Magda contemplated removing some of the Styrofoam from her rucksack, but that wasn't really going to help. So she didn't in the end. I think she would have been too embarrassed to face the other walkers if they knew she was travelling so lightly.

There was one small coffee shop in the village, and we commandeered a table outside. We sat for twenty minutes, then stood and pushed on. For a while the path was alright, then it got steep again. It was a long stretch that flanked one of the big hills of the ridge, and we went up diagonally across the range, finally getting to a col between two hills.

"Down now?" she asked hopefully.

It would never be that easy. The path turned sharply, then we began to ascend one of the two hills.

"The photo op is at the top," I said. "Then it is all knee-crunching downhill."

The climb took forty minutes, at the end of which even I was beginning to perspire. But finally a gentle breeze began to cool us. We walked around a turn in the path and the breeze intensified. Then we took the final turn and stepped onto the flat platform. The views were spectacular. Behind us we could see the flat plains leading to Pamplona and beyond. In front of us the ground fell away sharply, and about five kilometres away was a small town nestled in a valley. Our destination for the evening, Puente La Reine.

The platform was dominated by a huge modern sculpture. I looked at it in confusion. There seemed to be a tangle of rusted iron plates and triangles, connected by bars bent into weird and contorted shapes, as if a child had tried to construct an army out of chicken wire. After a few minutes, I thought I got it — Don Quixote tilting at the windmills. But the windmills looked a bit too human. And the figure of Don Quixote was as big as them; and he wasn't carrying a lance. Unless he was using it to lean on. Also, the Don Quixote story had nothing to do with this region of Spain.

Then I thought it might be a representation of the triumph of Christendom over the forces of Islam in the eleventh century. Either El Cid or the Holy Roman Emperor Charlemagne had defeated the Moors in a decisive battle quite close to this spot, and stopped the march of the Moors through Europe. That made more sense.

I turned to Magda. "Charlemagne defeating the Moors," I suggested.

"A ground of pilgrims defeating blisters and the hills," she replied. "You might be a great bodyguard, but you are a terrible judge of modern art."

I looked again. She could be right. In fact, it made a bit more sense, now that I looked carefully. What the leading figure was leaning on was not a lance, but a pilgrim staff. And the figures were all facing the same direction because no one was fighting anyone. They were marching. The direction they were facing was towards Santiago.

"Another interpretation," I continued, "is that the figures represent pilgrims doing the Camino. This being a part of the Camino and all."

"Good save," she muttered sarcastically.

We both faced the statues. Beyond them, I could see a small group of people, huddled together, and behind them two quad bikes. It was the other half of her crew — her director Amanda. With her were the cardinal and Inspector Rodriguez. I waved at the group. Someone waved back. With the position of the sun, overhead but behind them, I could not make out more than a silhouette.

"We better join them," Magda sighed.

"Hold up," shouted Mack nearby, pointing his camera. "Go back and do the final few metres again, and smile as you pass me."

He set up his camera, and with a scowl Magda complied. She turned and walked down the hill to the first bend, then around it. Then she turned and it was as if a new Magda had been beamed in in her place. Her smile was radiant. Her face was serene and calm. She strode up the final few metres, looked around, smiled in the direction of the camera without betraying the fact that she knew it was there, then turned and strode across the flat top of the ridge, towards the marching iron pilgrims.

"Always a pro," smiled Mack. "The things I have seen her smile through."

I followed her across the ridge, catching her easily. Now I could see who was in the group. The cardinal was in shorts and a nice short-sleeved shirt, looking casual. The inspector was starched and pristine — and smiling.

I smiled back. "You caught him?"

Rodriguez's smile wavered. "Not yet." Then he shrugged with continental indifference. "We are so far out of Pamplona now. We have nothing to fear from Mr Fleischmann."

Just then a shot rang out.

SIXTEEN

Like a panther, I pounced. I did it instinctively and without thought. I just reacted to the sound of the gun. Usain Bolt would not have been out of the blocks any faster than I was.

I dived across the space that separated me from Magda, hitting her in the waist, and rolling as I did so. I hit the ground first, with her on top of me. Then I rolled and she was underneath me, my body protecting her from the shots.

It is a myth that someone on top of you will protect you. They will add an element of cover, but if someone has a good rifle they can aim properly and shoot under you or around you, or find a gap where their target is exposed. And if they are using a proper sniper round, that doesn't really matter. Because if I was hit with a sniper round, it would pass right through my body and exit, losing very little velocity. Then it would hit Magda and take her out too. Hell, the Barret's M50 could take out the engine block of a jeep at a thousand yards. So me lying on top of Magda wasn't really providing much cover. It just ensured that she went down fast, and stayed down. But from my position the view was enchanting: the rolling hills, the deep valley, dark and mysterious.

I forced myself to look up from her cleavage. I scanned the surrounding countryside. A second shot rang out, and I flattened myself on top of her. The shot sounded very near. My eyes darted frantically.

Then another shot rang out, and another. Then about fifteen in rapid succession, and an acrid smell of burning sulphur wafted across the flat top of the ridge. I felt like a complete fool as the realisation struck. Someone was lighting firecrackers.

"Enjoying yourself?" Magda asked sarcastically. "You don't watch many of my movies. I am normally on top."

I got lightly to my feet, and stretched out a hand to help her up. Her back was covered in dust. She smiled that smile.

"Come up to my room tonight, big boy," she said with a wink. "We'll finish what you began."

The camera crew were running up to us, and both the inspector and the cardinal were in tow. They were all talking at once. The voice of Rodriguez cut through the babble.

"As I said, we have nothing to fear from Mr Fleischmann." His voice dripped disdain, and he had a superior smile on his face. *Chalk one up for the Spanish police*, he was thinking.

You let a dangerous lunatic with the hots for our bait get loose, I was thinking. But now was not the time to say that out loud.

I looked over to where a cloud of smoke was rapidly being dispersed by the strong breeze. A group of British students were grinning.

"Sorry, man," said one. "I didn't think you'd be that jumpy."

"Don't worry about it," I replied. I needn't have bothered. He quite clearly wasn't worried. He thought my dive was the funniest thing he had seen all day. One of the guys with him passed over a phone. They had obviously caught the whole thing on camera. I turned away before they could catch my glare. I didn't want to look sore about the whole thing. That would only add to their amusement.

I turned to Magda. "You alright?"

"No broken bones. I'll live."

"Well, if we are all done with our James Bond moment, we need to sit down and plan," said Rodriguez.

Planning. A complicated process. As far as Magda and her crew were concerned, we were security for her because her presence could provoke negative reactions. She had no awareness of the bait subplot. So when Magda was present, we had to plan for her personal protection. It was bodyguard work. But when she stepped away to discuss the day's filming with the crew, the second meeting took place: the one where we discussed exactly how we were going to place the bait in the trap, and how we were going to spring it if the bait was accepted. The real planning meeting, that the bait had no idea about.

Our plan was quite simple. We needed Magda in a quiet place near the trail, but not quite on it. And not when it was too busy. On the trail itself it would be too risky for someone to go after her. Off the trail presented the killer with an opportunity.

It was Cardinal Benoluchi who had come up with the perfect solution. There was a former nunnery about three kilometres off the main Camino route. It had been abandoned in the eighteenth century, and all that remained was a cloister and a small chapel. The chapel was disused and deconsecrated. I wasn't aware of how the deconsecration helped us, but it seemed an important point to Fermin. Some pilgrims took the detour to visit it, but not many. Occasional informal services were held there, but not often. To get to the chapel, you had to climb from our current position along a very rough trail, through scrub that changed to forestry when you got high enough.

"Ten years ago I did the Camino, and I remember visiting the ruins," he explained.

Our plan was for Magda to spend the day on the ridge, chatting to pilgrims as they passed. It would be good footage for her travelogue.

"We might even find one who will let me do him on camera," she said hopefully. I doubted it. Most of the pilgrims were Catholic, with an inherent sense of guilt. And there was no privacy. They were hardly going to go behind a bush to do the deed.

After her Camino meet-and-greet ended, we would make our way along the trail to the nunnery, where we would camp out for the night.

Of course, a secret plan is no good unless everyone knows about it. That was Magda's department. Without asking, without realising how important it was for us, she took out her phone and began working the social networks. Pictures of her chatting with pilgrims went straight onto her Facebook and Instagram pages. She flashed, much to the cardinal's disapproval. That one went on Twitter. They don't have the same rigorous community standards on Twitter, apparently. It is a well-known platform for distributing and promoting porn, which surprised me very much.

The hits began to build up quickly. The Likes and the Shares grew as the afternoon stretched. Around three, Magda got tired of her filmed interviews and took a while to herself. She spread a blanket on the ground in the lee of a small rise. The rise blocked the wind, and the stop was a sun trap. She sat on the blanket and took off her hiking boots. Then she pulled off her T-shirt. She loosened her pants and rolled them off her legs. Then she reached behind her back and elegantly snapped a clasp. Her bra fell free. She laid it beside her T-shirt and stretched out, closing her eyes. She was wearing nothing but skimpy black panties. The rise she was using for shelter could have provided privacy, but she had carefully positioned her blanket so that she was hard to miss from the pilgrim route. Amanda positioned herself on a tree stump nearby, and encouraged a procession of people to take a secret snap. Most opted for selfies. For some reason, including themselves in the shot seemed to remove an element of smut about the proceeding, at least in the minds of the pilgrims who paused. Amanda, monitoring the social media, was almost wetting herself. This was becoming a cyberspace event.

I watched the cardinal with wry amusement. When Magda had first spread out her blanket he had been chatting urbanely to her, the picture of comfort. But when the clothes had started to come off he had got progressively less comfortable, finally muttering: "Tongues will wag if my colleagues in Rome find out about this."

He had turned away and stared into the distance, as if contemplating an uncertain future. Or storing the image of the topless Magda in his memory for future recall? I don't know what goes on in the head of a cardinal.

Around four, Magda stood up from the blanket and strode over to her crew. She stood chatting to them for about ten minutes, as she sipped a mug of coffee. She posed for a few more photographs. Then she strode over to her clothes, and got dressed again. "That will be great for promoting the travel documentary. It will get people talking," she said. Amanda nodded enthusiastically.

I nodded too. But I wasn't thinking of the ratings for her film. I was thinking that every perv in northern Spain now knew that Magda Lynn was going to be spending the night sleeping under the stars just a few miles off the regular trail.

The bait had been set. It just remained to be seen if our quarry would try to take it.

SEVENTEEN

At six we set off. Magda was adamant she would not walk any further. She would travel on one of the two quad bikes that had brought the cardinal, the inspector, and her film crew up to the top of the ridge. There were no roads.

Her decision meant the cleric or the cop would have to leg it. Fermin looked at Rodriguez and sighed. He turned to me and whispered: "Can you see that popinjay walk in the heat?"

I laughed. He had the guy pegged accurately. He was suited for a beat that took in a fashionable boulevard in a sophisticated city, not a dusty forest trail.

So Rodriguez took the wheel and Magda sat beside him. She looked at me beseechingly, but I grinned. *Don't walk, take the consequences.*

I noticed the inspector placing a hand on her knee as he made some remark. She lifted his hand and placed it back on the wheel. A moment later, it had strayed again.

The cardinal sighed. "He hasn't a hope. He is not her type. You, perhaps. Me, when I was younger. But no, I mustn't think about such things. Celibacy is a vocation, not a curse. Celibacy is a vocation, not a curse. I must keep repeating the mantra." He smiled at me. "Let's walk."

And he strode out with a long and confident step. After a few hundred yards, he turned and said: "I must do the Camino again. The way of the pilgrim suits me."

We walked on in companionable silence, enjoying the fresh air, the views, and the warmth of the early evening. The scents of the forest wafted gently towards us, and birdsong filled the air. The drone of the quad engines was not loud enough to spoil the evening.

We walked for perhaps fifteen minutes. We had reached the edge of the forest and the foliage had thickened considerably. The trail we were following had dwindled to a single-file track. The two quads were parked up, blocking the way ahead. Magda had a red face, and was not happy.

"They say they can't go any further," she snarled. "They say I have to walk."

"They say right," I confirmed. "The trail is not wide enough for quads. From here on, we travel as nature intended."

"Not me," she said. "I want to camp here for the night."

There were a number of problems with that plan. Her production company would lose their valuable shots. There was no clearing here, but there was at the nunnery. But the biggest objection — the one I could not say to her — was that a trap only worked if the bait was in place.

I could have argued. Instead, I heaved one of the big sacks from the back of a quad onto my back. It was the camping gear. Fermin lifted the other bag — food and other provisions — onto his shoulders. Of one mind without the need for discussion, we clambered over the quads and plunged onto the trail ahead. Magda had to follow — or sleep out in the rough. Problem solved without a debate.

After a very short wait, we heard the sounds of pursuit. First came the cameraman and director. Then Magda, cursing softly. Finally, a good way behind, the inspector joined the convoy.

"This is the shit, the absolute shit," I heard him cry up the path towards us. "There is no pavement."

We had a little over two kilometres to walk, so I don't know what the problem was. The path was narrow and overgrown, but very manageable. And the heat had gone out of the day. It was pleasant. I had taken far worse walks in the past, like the time I had traversed a cliff path with a hitwoman disguised as a nun taking pot shots at me. After that, this was easy.

But thinking back on that murderous nun, I was on alert to what might lie ahead. This was ideal ambush country. From what we knew about the killer we were stalking, he took his victims in secret. None were snatched while they were in company. So, in theory Magda was safe as long as she kept up. And the inspector was the last in the line, so she was keeping up. She was not the loose sheep at the back of the flock. She should be safe. But we also knew our killer mixed things up. He did not have an MO when it came to dispatching his victims. So our presence might not be the deterrent I hoped.

That kept me alert. I made sure I was first on the trail, with Fermin behind me. If someone had passed through in the last few days, I would read the signs. There would be broken branches, trampled vegetation. There was nothing. This was clearly not a popular diversion off the Camino, and no one had taken it for a while.

The thing about a trail is, if you know the first kilometre is clear, you can pretty much guarantee the second kilometre is free. Like a good book, you start at the start. Someone could not mysteriously appear halfway along. Carl Lewis was a great long-jumper, but even he couldn't jump a kilometre into the woods and take up his walk from there. So after a few hundred metres, I relaxed. I would resume my vigilance as we approached the nunnery, because our killer could always have reached the spot from a different angle.

He hadn't.

The path opened out onto a flat clearing nestled in the side of a steep hill. We were surrounded by forest. The centre of the clearing was dominated by a stone chapel, in the characteristic yellow sandstone of the region. The pillars of a cloister were still visible in front of the chapel, where the nuns could have strolled in the evening air, reading their office as they enjoyed the view. But all the outbuildings were gone. They were probably wooden and had not lasted the test of the centuries. Beyond, the trail petered out. There was just the wall of trees that marked the resumption of forestry.

As the others set up camp, I walked forward and explored the edges of the wood. There was no sign that anyone had been here, beyond an empty soup tin that looked years old, and the remains of a small campfire of similar vintage.

I strolled back. "The site is secure," I said.

"Darling, you worry too much," said Magda. If only she knew.

While I was gone, they had set up four tents and someone had laid out a gas camping cooker and a throw-away barbecue. Magda was in one of the middle tents, with her director. The inspector had a tent of his own. Cameraman Mack occupied the third tent with his film gear, while Fermin and I had the final one, the one nearest the trail head. Of all the people I could have shared a tent with, he was probably the best company. And he seemed to be an outdoors man. I had no complaints.

"How safe is it?" he whispered.

"We are assuming our man is not a sniper," I replied, "and it would give him no sick thrill to take out the tents from a distance. So that is not a worry. As I see it, he can sneak up and try to take Magda during the night, or he can provide a distraction to break us up, then pick her off. Or we might be misreading the situation completely, in which case we get up in the morning and eat a good breakfast, then walk on."

Fermin did not look happy. "A part of me is terrified about what might happen tonight. I am not a man of action, like yourself and Rodriguez. But a bigger part of me wants this over, and the route safe for pilgrims for years to come. So, here's to a really horrible night."

EIGHTEEN

My eyes snapped open. It was as dark as the depths of hell, and silent as the tomb. What had woken me?

I listened. Nothing. Not a sound on the night air. I sniffed. Nothing. The nose is not something to rely on in surveillance, but sometimes you get a whiff of aftershave or stale cigarette smoke, which tells you someone new has entered the scene. I was picking up nothing.

Without making a noise, barely moving, I slid my hand up towards my inflatable pillow. My fingers reached out and touched metal. My hand closed on the throw-down pistol. A tiny weapon with only six shots. But oiled, loaded, and ready for action. I slid the safety to off, and waited.

There! That was it. The sound of someone moving at the periphery of the camp. God, what I wouldn't give for night vision scopes right now.

I slid out of my sleeping bag and put on my boots, lacing them quickly. Then I slipped out of the tent. I had left it open for just such an emergency. The cardinal stirred beside me, but didn't wake. He was getting the bad night he wanted.

I kept low, slithering from the tent without disturbing the flap. No need to signal my position. Prone, I scanned the ground before me. There was a three-quarter moon out, which helped enormously. I spotted the intruder quickly. Oddly, he was not crouching, making no effort to conceal himself. He was standing at full height, and was over near where we had dug our latrine earlier. It was Inspector Rodriguez.

I stood and walked towards him, slipping the safety on my pistol back on. "You startled me," I said.

He jumped, then realised it was only me. I was amused to see he had dressed fully just to take a piss. Earlier, he had gone to bed in silk pyjamas. The guy really was not the outdoors type. Camping was new territory for him.

"Call of nature," he explained.

"And you got dressed for that?"

"But of course. And you would not?"

I didn't even bother to answer.

"Goodnight," I said, and I turned back towards my tent. I scanned the horizon as I walked, more habit than a real check. Nothing. Of course.

As I got to the tent, Magda stirred in the tent beside mine.

"Nothing to worry about," I whispered. "Just our dear inspector taking a leak. He got dressed to piss, can you believe that?"

"Anything you say, love. Oh, that feels good," she murmured.

I was puzzled for a minute, then I realised she was dreaming. I might as well have been whispering to the trees.

I got back into my tent. The cardinal was gently snoring. I pulled the flap across, but I felt slightly unsettled. I think I had woken up at the wrong point of my sleep cycle. That can throw a man. Or the sight of the inspector dressing to use the latrine might have offended my sensibilities as a camper. Or perhaps I have a sixth sense for danger, and it was pinging just below the level of awareness. I don't know. I do know that I was suddenly not tired. I knew I was not going to settle easily to sleep. I would get into the sleeping bag, snuggle up warm and cosy, and spend the next hour listening to bloody insects outside. Insects annoy me on so many levels. Take the humble fly, for instance. The bastard breathes through its belly. They don't have lungs. They have a tube in their belly leading into their abdomen, and the oxygen just diffuses throughout their body through a system of little tubes. So that means that even if you could catch the blighter, you couldn't put your hands around its neck and strangle the life out of it.

Those are the sort of dark — and trivial — thoughts that fly through my head in the middle of the night when sleep eludes me. And I wasn't opening that Pandora's Box. So I pulled on a light jacket, left my boots on, and lay on top of the sleeping bag, and began to focus on my breath. A little bit of mindfulness would get me through the night.

I kept my eyes open but defocused, and scanned my body. All was comfortable. Then I began to follow my breath, in and out. In and out. In and out. Ignoring the thoughts that arose.

Damn those insects. How I'd love to get my hands on their...

Then back to the breath, in and out.

After a while, my mind calmed and went deliciously blank. The process was working. I lay on my back, vaguely aware of the gentle snoring of the cardinal, the drone of the night life outside, the rustle of the breeze in the trees, the snap of a twig...

The snap of a twig?

The snap of a twig was definitely not right. I sat up, instantly alert. Silence for thirty seconds.

Then...

A shot rang out. And this time there was no doubt. It was not a firecracker.

NINETEEN

I hit the cardinal in the ribs, hard.

"Keep your head down, and get dressed."

The shot had woken him, and he nodded quietly. He didn't say anything. His face was pale but resolute. Then he whispered: "In or out, when I am dressed?"

"Out and away from the tent, because it is too easy a target. But stay low. Crawl."

I was pulling on my pants as I gave him his instructions. Then I was out and moving fast, taking my weight on my elbows and knees, slithering in the best army fashion. I headed towards the remains of the fire, around which we had sat with our dinner. The fire had gone out, but the ashes were warm. Beside the fire was the gas stove. I prayed the matches would still be there. They were.

I pulled the gas bottle from the stove and heard the satisfying hiss of escaping propane. I dropped the small canister upside down in the middle of the warm ashes, the gas streaming out on all sides and rising into the air, the smell filling my lungs. By a mystery of chemistry, the escaping gas cooled the canister and it felt freezing. I struck a match and dropped it right in the centre, rolling quickly away.

There was a whoosh and the night sky lit up like bright day. You could have read a newspaper by the flickering light.

I knew that made us all a target, but it also would have blinded anyone watching us with night vision goggles. Bit of a toss-up, but I felt it was the right first response. Even if the guy was not using goggles, whatever adjustment his eyes had made to the dark would be wiped out by the sudden flare. Of course, our adjustment to the dark would also be screwed. But we weren't the ones trying to aim a sniper rifle.

I rolled rapidly away from the fire and slithered towards Fermin, who was crouching low but looking confused.

"Get under the trees, and I'll be over in a minute with the others."

He nodded and moved quickly. He had a level head. Good to know.

Just then I heard a voice, and turned to see Mack emerge from his tent and stand up straight, looking around him. He was rubbing the sleep from his eyes.

"What's the story, mate?" he called. "I heard a noise."

"Someone is shooting at us, you fool! Get under the trees."

His eyes opened like saucers, and he began running towards where the cardinal was frantically waving. He didn't even try to crouch, but he wasn't the target so I didn't worry. I hurried to the tent Magda and Amanda were sharing. Both were wide awake, sitting up, and terrified.

"Grab your clothes and run for the trees. And keep low," I hissed. I had to repeat it before they both started moving. A moment later they exited the tent, and as they did a second shot whizzed past, missing me by a whisker. The flames hadn't blinded our shooter for long.

It took nerve, but I stood and spread my arms to draw his fire. Then I ran towards the clearing, away from the edge of the forest. After a couple of steps I dropped and rolled backwards, then slithered back towards the trees. As I did, another shot rang out and I heard the *thunk* as it struck the ground. It has missed me by a country mile. He had anticipated my movement and shot ahead of me, but I was now moving in a different direction. The ruse had given the two girls a chance to get to cover.

It didn't take me long to slither across to them. Fermin had moved everyone back from the treeline into deeper cover and was peering anxiously back towards me. He had instinctively taken charge.

"All safe and accounted for," he whispered. He wasn't fazed by the fact Magda and Amanda were hastily dressing in front of him, but Mack was furtively taking in the sight.

"Does everyone have their shoes?" I asked.

"No, mate. I left mine in the tent," said Mack.

"What size are you?" whispered Fermin.

"Eleven, mate. I mean, Your Eminence, mate."

"I'm ten, so my evening shoes might fit you."

Most hikers bring a pair of sneakers or sandals with them for the evenings. After marching for thirty kilometres, it is a huge relief to take off the boots. It can be the highlight of your day. I was impressed that the cardinal had thought to remove his bag from the tent when he had fled a few minutes earlier. I watched as he fished inside, and emerged with a pair of navy canvas loafers. Mack didn't look happy as he squeezed his boat-like feet into them, but it was better than trying to make his escape barefoot. And no one was volunteering to walk across the open space to his tent to fetch his boots.

I didn't know where to start. Magda was intelligent enough to suspect that she had got the co-operation of the Church on her movie project at a cost. But she would not have known that she was bait in a game of cat and mouse. And her director and cameraman were clueless. I would have to think through what I was about to say carefully.

"Somebody is shooting at us," I began. State the bleeding obvious. "And we know it is not some night hunter making a mistake, because he kept firing at us after the campfire was relit. We are going to proceed on the basis this is a planned attack, rather than a random one. So the shooter has a target. I'm guessing Magda."

Nobody demurred. On many levels it made sense, even if you did not have my inside information. She was the celebrity. She was the pornographer sullying the pilgrimage. She was the scarlet woman.

The cardinal nodded. "I agree," he said. That seemed to settle it.

"Here's my plan," I said. "The inspector and I will stay with Magda, to protect her. Both of us are armed, trained professionals. But we are going to split up, because there is no point in everyone being in danger."

I turned to the cardinal.

"Fermin, I want you to lead Mack and Amanda up the hill through the forest, then back onto the trail and get them to safety. It will take you a few hours, but if the gunman is following us, you should have no problems."

I turned to the inspector.

"We are going to lead the shooter further down the trail, and hopefully set an ambush for him. But our priority is to keep Magda safe."

He grinned ruefully. "I should have used steel cuffs," he said.

I wasn't so sure that Terrance Fleischmann was our assailant. He seemed more fixated on Magda than the Camino, and I didn't believe he was our serial killer. But I had been a detective now for about two days. What did I know? Rodriguez might be right. He was an incompetent arresting officer, but he might be a great investigator. Certainly someone was after us, and it could have been Fleischmann as easily as anyone else.

I sighed. Now came the difficult part. None of them were going to like this. "We have to let him know we have split up. And we have to let him know which group to follow."

They looked at me blankly. Clearly I would have to spell it out.

"Once we are organised, Magda needs to stand up and run across the clearing towards the rear of the nunnery, where the trail continues. She needs to be seen by him. Rodriguez and I will go with her, and three of us will disappear down the trail. That's your cue to make some noise as you head up the hill through the forest."

"He will try to kill me!" said Magda, going white.

"No. He might shoot at me or Rodriguez, but not at you. You are his target. If he had just wanted to kill you, he would have done so by now. He wants to hunt you. Well, we are going to turn the situation around and hunt him instead."

TWENTY

Cardinal Benoluchi quickly took charge of his companions. I didn't envy him. Mack was young and fit, but clearly in a funk. Amanda was an indoors city girl. He would have his work cut out. But as I watched him methodically check that they were all prepared, and sort through his own gear, I knew they were in safe hands. He might be shoving on in years, but there was granite flowing through his veins.

He looked at me and smiled tightly. "I will keep them safe," he said.

"I know you will."

I turned to Rodriguez. He was ready. Fully dressed, fully booted. As if he had just stepped out of the tent to take a piss. His fastidiousness meant he had not made the mistake of leaving anything useful in the tent, as Mack had.

"Weapon?"

"Service revolver," he said, patting his belt, where I could see it hanging. "Full magazine."

"And...?"

"That's it. I brought no spares."

My heart sank a little, but I forced myself not to show it. This was my territory now. Manhunting was what I was good at. I would make this work.

I was as heavily armed as the circumstances allowed, with the inspector's half-empty throw-down gun and a hunter's knife. I scanned Magda from head to toe. She was dressed in shorts and a white T-shirt, with boots and socks. She would survive the warm night out in the open, but there is little stopping power in cotton. This was going to be risky.

"Ready?"

She nodded. She looked less ready than resigned. She took a few deep breaths, then nodded again. "I'm ready."

It was on.

I dropped on my belly and slithered out of the trees. Like being back on the assault course in basic training, only without the net overhead to impede my progress. My elbows weren't as hardened as they used to be, but I wouldn't be out there long. Making progress on your belly is quite easy. Raise your torso an inch or two off the ground with your elbows, bring one leg up until your hip is perpendicular to your body but still on the ground, then push forward from that leg. A bit like doing half a breaststroke, and not much faster. It must have taken a full two minutes to cross the clearing, through our abandoned tents, and on to the edge of the trail leading past the nunnery and on through the forest. Progress was slow, but steady and silent.

When I got to the trailhead, I turned and looked back. They could not see me in the dark. But that didn't matter. Fermin's instructions were to wait exactly three minutes, then send Magda out.

I waited, counting the seconds in my head. Suddenly there was a movement and Magda came out across the clearing, bent low at the waist. She was running quickly but her speed was compromised by her low crouch. She got to the centre of the camp and suddenly straightened and slowed down. She turned to look in the direction of the shooter, then abruptly sped up again, diving onto the ground just beyond me.

She was followed by the inspector, who ran quickly at a half crouch. He was nearly in cover when a shot rang out and leaves rustled as the bullet passed perilously close to us. He swore, but kept running and reached cover safely.

I risked rising slightly, and fired blindly towards the shooter. It was a waste of a precious bullet, but it let him know where we were and where we were going. That was important. He needed to chase us. You can't lead someone into a trap unless they are following you.

As soon as I had fired the shot, I grabbed Magda by the arm and plunged into the trail. The moonlight helped, but the foliage blocked so much of the light we were stumbling like blind people. Rodriguez was behind us, breathing heavily.

"The bastard nearly killed me," he wheezed.

"No fear of that," I said. "He's a poor shot. If he can, he will take you and me out, so that he can concentrate on Magda. But it won't be from long range with that rifle. He's an amateur shot."

That was a wild assumption on my part. I knew he was using a hunting rifle because I had heard three shots now. I cannot identify every type of rifle from the noise of its discharge. But if he had been using a sniper rifle, there would have been a bigger bang and a sonic boom as the bullets whizzed past. If he had been using a suppressor to muffle the sound, there would have been a soft bang and a sonic boom, the distinctive sharp crack. The discharge had been neither soft nor loud, so I knew he was not using a high-powered weapon. And there was no sonic boom.

I also knew he was a bad shot, or thought I knew. He had fired and missed with the shot that woke us up. Then he had missed me as I ran for cover. Now he had missed the inspector. If he was the Camino Killer, we knew he liked to get up close and personal with his prey. He would only become truly dangerous when he got in range. But once he was close to us, I was close to him. Then the fun would begin.

I hoped Fermin was doing his bit. He had to make as much noise as possible, then begin climbing up the ridge away from the clearing. That would alert the shooter to the fact our party had split up. I was betting everything on him following us rather than the cardinal. And I reckoned he would not risk starting his pursuit until he knew the second party was gone. So we had a good head start on him. I had to get Magda as far up the trail as I could, until I found a suitable place to spring an ambush.

The problem was, I didn't know where I was going, and I had no plan.

TWENTY-ONE

For perhaps thirty minutes, we moved as rapidly as we could along the path. And by as rapidly as we could, I mean we moved at a snail's pace. The problem was that it was dark. We didn't want to risk using a flashlight because it would be very easy to follow us. And besides, we didn't have a flashlight. I'm sure that was a factor in our decision to fumble in the darkness.

Magda was not used to hiking. I knew that from the previous afternoon. What I didn't realise was that Rodriguez was also not used to it. He was in a constant state of stress because of what the branches and brambles were doing to his precious trouser crease. He viewed nature as an inconvenience designed to spoil the way his clothes hung.

Eventually I snapped at Magda: "Give him one of your tampons. I think he's on his period."

Rodriguez stopped for a minute, then glared daggers at me when he resumed marching. I could feel his eyes boring into the back of my head. I didn't care.

Normally a night hike is fun. I remember them from my scout days as a teen. But back then, every other member of the troop wanted to be there. And no one was following us with a gun, so perhaps the comparison was not apt.

After a while, we got into a rhythm. It only takes a minute or so for your eyes to partially adjust to the darkness, and less than five for complete adjustment. The pupils dilate to the max, allowing whatever scattered light is out there to enter the eyeball. The rods and cones adjust to firing under the reduced stimulus. Inky blackness resolves itself into patches of true dark, and patches where you know there is something because the darkness feels less thick. Finally, we began to make out vague shapes, and the path became easier to pick out. I am not saying our speed picked up, but there was less cursing from Rodriguez, and Magda was breathing easier and breaking less branches.

We walked on in hostile silence. The only noises breaking the peace were the crunch of our footsteps on the clay and the swish of the branches as they were pushed aside. And the inspector's growls as thorns snagged on his pristine shirt.

In times of stress, it is vital to keep spirits up. I was not worried about Rodriguez. He was a professional, and he would just have to man up. But Magda was not a professional, and I had been hired to make sure she stayed alive. Mother Church did not want anyone dying on my watch, if it could be prevented. So I had a duty of care to her. I decided to take her mind off our desperate flight.

"My brother sent me a worrying text message," I whispered.

"What?" She was startled, but I noticed her stride lengthened slightly as she caught my words. I took that as a good sign.

"Yeah — he wants me to book him a trip up Mount Toubkal."

"Mount what?"

"It's a mountain in Africa."

"I thought Kilimanjaro was the mountain in Africa?"

"It's a big place. There's more than one mountain."

"Really?"

Chalk one strike against the Polish education system.

"Yes, really. And he wants to climb it."

"So let him." She seemed to be losing interest in the conversation.

"You see, he wants to climb it with Serena."

"I am happy for them," she said. But from her tone I had my doubts.

"He's not married to Serena."

"I'm sure he is old enough to make those decisions for himself. What business is it of yours?"

"None, I suppose. It's just, I don't think his wife will be too happy about it. And I like his wife. More than I like him, in fact. She's not a pain in the butt."

Her eyes lit up. I could feel it in the darkness. I had her hooked. This was the distraction that would keep her marching.

"Okay," she whispered, a tone of uncertainty in her voice. "I don't know what else to say. I don't know your brother at all."

Fair point.

"He's all right. A bit of a fusspot, the sort of guy who waits for a green man to cross the road, but not all bad."

"Everyone waits for the green man to cross the road," came the voice of Rodriguez, who had obviously tuned into our conversation. I turned to Magda and raised an eyebrow. The gesture was lost in the darkness. Then Magda let me down.

"The inspector is right. Who doesn't wait for the green man?"

Am I the only man who plays dodgeball with the traffic? Surely not.

"What I mean is, he is a stickler for the rules. Does things by the book. Lives his life as if it was a problem in actuarial accounting. He has a terrible fear of doing anything that is not completely respectable. Which is why this text is so out of character."

Survival in my line depends on finely tuned instincts and senses that are always on a knife-edge. I could hear the rhythm of Rodriguez's breathing, and it changed. It softened and regularised. He had tuned out of our conversation. Still, I was talking to Magda to keep her calm, not to actually get advice on my brother and his complicated love life. I didn't need to keep Rodriguez calm; he was a cop. That came with the territory.

"Why is it out of character?" asked Magda, taking the bait.

"He's a happily married man. He wouldn't stray. Even if the chance arose, it wouldn't be in his character. He just wouldn't. And on top of that, no one would fancy him, so the chance wouldn't arise."

That last may have been a little malicious. He's not the worst. But Lester is no charmer. Whoever Serena was, she was unlikely to have pursued him.

"So let me get this straight. Your brother wants to spend a holiday in Morocco with a woman who is not his wife, and he has asked you to organise it for him. And you are wondering how to handle it?"

"Yes."

"I suppose you are wondering if they are sleeping together?"

That was exactly what I was wondering.

"They are climbing a mountain," she said. "That's tough work. It's no romantic break. If they just wanted to fool around, they would have chosen a beach holiday, or gone on a city break. Romantic dinners, sunsets, that vibe. But he is climbing a mountain, so I think we can assume sex is off the table."

"Really?" I heaved a sigh of relief.

"No, you fool. If he is going on holiday with a woman who is not his wife, he is banging her. What planet did you fall from?"

I was silent for a few minutes as we continued to work our way along the dark path.

"Why has he asked you to organise the trip?"

"I've told my family that I work as an adventure holiday specialist. They think it is what I do for a living."

She let out a low whistle. "You mean, they don't know you work in private security?"

I could hear the incredulity in her voice. But what was I meant to do? Casually drop it into the dinner conversation over the Christmas turkey: *By the way, I kill people for a living. Can you pass the cranberry sauce?* I went on the defensive.

"Does your family know what you do for a living?"

"Of course. They fully support me. In fact, my mother runs my fan club. After she divorced Dad, she even road tested a few of my co-stars, just to get back into the dating game."

I was getting out of my depth here. Human emotions are a minefield I try to avoid. Fortunately, the inspector came to my rescue.

"Who the hell cares? My pants will be ruined from all the thorns."

The path had been getting easier for some time, and now it was quite straight and reasonably flat underfoot. I could sense the topography of the ground changing too. We had started with a forest trail. Now I felt we were skirting the side of the hill. To our left, the ground fell away steeply, almost sheer in parts. I could see out through the thinning tree cover over the valley below. But to our right, the vegetation was as dense as ever, rising up towards the ridge above us. In a word, the terrain was narrowing from a flat expanse to a narrow strip flanking a hill. And when a route funnels, that is the perfect site for an ambush. I began to pay more active attention to the surroundings. But no matter how careful you are, you can always get caught.

I heard it first, then felt it. A soft splash, then water seeping over the top of my shoe and drenching my sock. It seeped between my toes and sloshed up my ankle. I braked suddenly, only just stopping my other foot from sinking into the stream.

"Shit," I muttered. Then Magda, who had not applied the brakes, ran into my back and my other foot plunged into the cold water.

"Shit," I muttered again. Some messages bear repetition.

"What's wrong?"

"Just stepped into a stream."

I really should have heard it. It was deep enough — up to my knees — but moving slowly. And we were making noise coming through the woods. So perhaps not my fault. I stepped through and stood on the other side. Magda took my outstretched hand and stepped over to join me. Rodriguez lengthened his stride and stepped across. The three of us stood in an uneasy huddle for a minute. Then Magda, in a quiet voice, said: "In all the panic, I never thought of it. We should ring the police."

Very good advice. But easier said than done.

"Do you have a phone?" I asked. I could vaguely see the white blob of her face crumble.

"I left it in the tent."

I felt a small smile seeping through my stoic features as I prepared to tell the white lie: that I had done the same. Then I realised it was true. My phone — a high-powered satellite phone with built-in computer, disguised as a regular smartphone — was in my rucksack. And my rucksack was back in the tent. Rookie mistake. I had remembered the little pistol, but I had left behind a valuable source of communication.

True, I had no intention of calling in the cavalry. I needed our shooter to follow us so that I could lure him into a trap and capture him. If he ran now, he would be off the mountain and miles away by the time help arrived. So I had deliberately never suggested phoning for help. But Magda knew none of that.

Then Rodriguez spoke. "I have my phone."

"I could kiss you," said Magda.

"Un momento," he said. I could hear the note of gallantry in his voice. "It is in my pocket."

He reached in and took out the phone. I prayed for poor reception.

He held it up with a flourish, gently gripped between his thumb and forefinger. For a moment it stood there at face level, then the phone began to slip. Unpanicked, Rodriguez lifted his other hand to grab it. It was then that I deliberately stumbled and bumped into him. The phone fell out of his grasp and plopped into the water.

Magda gasped in shock. Straight away, the inspector stooped and put a hand in the water, up to his elbow. He swished it around for a while, eventually grunting in satisfaction. He pulled the phone out of the water and held it out triumphantly.

"Got you," he said. He tapped the screen. "It must have switched off with the fall," he said. He pressed the button at the side before either of us could stop him. There was a tiny flash, then nothing. The screen did not power up.

"You've blown it," said Magda. "Now we are on our own."

TWENTY-TWO

An owl hooted and Rodriguez jumped. I looked at my two companions in the darkness. Magda seemed to be holding up better. The gumshoe seemed a little on edge. Almost like he wasn't used to being hunted down like a human target.

And now the phone was gone. That was a disaster, if you were Magda. Or the perfect outcome, if you were me. I didn't want a police chopper swooping in and scaring off our killer. We had a shot tonight at ending this. I really felt it. All I had to do was keep Magda out of the firing line.

I said: "Don't worry. Cardinal Benoluchi will have phoned for help. The cavalry is on the way."

Not strictly true. Fermin and I had had a quick discussion before we began our dash, and I had warned him to make sure no one phoned for help for at least two hours. Only then was he to phone in our rescue. He had been reluctant, but he had understood. We were both here to do a job. The killer had to be caught.

I thought of his task. He had to climb through the forest to the top of the ridge with Mack and Amanda, then drop back to the path which would lead to the ridge and the modern sculpture of the pilgrims. That should keep him out of the way of our killer, and keep all three safe. I trusted Fermin. There was something about him.

That left us pushing forward and baiting the trap.

Looking around me, this spot felt right. Once we cleared the little stream, the path opened up. The forest ended for a while, at least on the downhill side. And the drop down the hill steepened until it was almost a cliff. But on the uphill side the trees were still thick, once you crossed the ditch into cover. We could make a stand here.

I outlined my idea quickly. "Rodriguez, you follow the stream about ten metres into the trees and wait. Get behind a tree. Don't just crouch down in the leaves."

This was important. I suspected that our stalker was using night vision goggles. The question was, which sort? If he was using regular goggles, they would enhance whatever light was there. Even a twinkling star might be enough to illuminate the track like a flare. But you could hide from those goggles by simply dropping out of sight, just like you could hide from regular binoculars. Behind a bush or prone on the ground would do.

But there was an outside chance he had the other sort of goggles: infrared night vision. These worked not by enhancing the existing light, but by using a different form of light entirely. They sought out temperature differences. The view they gave was a lot less crisp and clear than the regular goggles, but a lot harder to hide from. Infrared picked up body heat. So even if you concealed yourself behind a bush, the heat of your body would light up that spot like the fourth of July. Rodriguez would have to wait behind something substantial, like a tree or a rock. Then, when he heard the sound of the killer passing, he was to come out and get behind him, trapping him in a kill zone.

Magda and I would move further along the trail, and I would get her safely hidden up a tree. Then I would scurry forward as far as I could and light a small fire. That would make it look like we believed we had evaded him, and were regrouping for the remainder of the night. He would pass the inspector's position and advance towards me. The inspector would close in behind him, and I would jump him from the front. The path was narrow enough that I might be able to get right up close and bring him down without a shot being fired. What could go wrong? Rodriguez, for a start.

"You want me to wade through the river? In cream chinos?"

TWENTY-THREE

I looked at him in disgust. How had this popinjay ever risen above traffic duty?

The ground was muddy. I reached down and dug into the clay with my fingers, then smeared a streak of dark brown gunge down his trouser leg. I repeated the outrage on his clean shirt.

"You have nothing to worry about — your clothes need a wash anyway, so it doesn't matter if you get them dirty. Now get into that forest and get under cover before I get really pissed off."

His eyes narrowed and hardened, and his face went pale. For a moment, I thought he was going to hit me. I almost wanted it. But no. He took a deep breath, got his feelings under control, and walked away from me. He scrambled along the edge of the stream into the woods, and got behind a fallen trunk. He squatted down.

"You'll need to get lower than that if he has night vision goggles," I sneered. Then I turned and walked away, further up the path.

Magda scrambled after me. "That was a bit harsh," she whispered.

"Was it?"

After a moment, she replied. "No. He was asking for it."

We walked on silently, for about fifty metres.

"Will he do his bit?"

"I hope so," I replied. "Ideally we want the killer in a trap. We don't want him to be able to retreat. If it goes well, this ends tonight."

"What ends tonight?"

I kept forgetting: Magda did not realise she was the bait in a trap. I said nothing.

This spot looked as good as any other. Better than most. I stopped and looked around. There was a thick trunk just off the path that branched about two metres above the ground. The geometry of the tree was perfect. The thick limb branched off towards the forest and slightly forward of the way we were travelling. That meant that if I could get Magda up there, she could sit on the limb and the main trunk of the tree would hide her from anyone coming up the trail after us. She would be safe.

I looked at the tree. She looked at the tree.

"You want me up there?"

I nodded, then bent down and cupped my hands to give her a boost. She ignored my hands and straightened, leaping slightly to catch an overhanging branch with one hand. Gracefully she swung her body up until a foot touched the trunk about a metre off the ground. Her body twisted slightly, and her other foot came to rest on the fork of the tree. Her second hand came up and gripped another branch, and in a twinkle she was seated comfortably on the tree limb, completely hidden from the path.

"How did you do that?" I was impressed.

"I was a gymnast as a child. How do you think I can get into all the extreme positions in my movies?"

Not being familiar with her oeuvre, I didn't answer that. Instead, I said: "Stay there until I come back for you, or the cops arrive to rescue you. Don't come out for anyone else."

And then I was off, jogging along the trail in the dim light. I ran in a sort of mincing stride, lifting my legs high and stepping gingerly. Low branches and creepers would not stop me. In a few minutes, I had advanced almost three hundred metres and had reached a proper clearing. It was perfect. Quickly I scrambled around and gathered twigs as kindling. Then I put a tepee of small branches around them. Finally I found a long rotting branch and snapped it. I had to put more weight on it than I thought, and the snap cracked out like a rifle shot in the darkness. The sound would have carried for miles.

I didn't panic. I needed him to think we were far up the trail. I hadn't intended the loud crack, but if our pursuer heard it, that might be a good thing. And as it was done now, there was no point worrying.

I searched my pockets. I still felt foolish about leaving my phone behind at the campsite. But I had not travelled completely empty-handed. I had remembered my gun. I had remembered my wallet (fat good it would do me in the woods). And I had remembered to throw a small butane lighter into my pocket. I thumbed the flint and applied the tiny flame to the kindling. It caught immediately. I blew gently, nursing the spark into a flame. The twigs were dry, and in a moment I heard the satisfying crackling sound as they began to burn. Soon I would have a pleasant campfire. Excellent.

The ground around the fire seemed to be clear. I didn't want this licking up and starting a forest inferno, but it looked safe enough to leave unattended. Quickly I turned and began jogging back along the trail towards Magda and the inspector. I hoped I was fast enough.

I had faith in my feet by now. So I moved swiftly. Too swiftly, as it turned out. A bramble on the path caught my instep and I felt my body tumble. I threw my arms forward and got my palms in front of my face. I snapped my head to the side so my face wouldn't slam into the ground. Preserve those features at any cost!

I crashed to the ground and felt a searing pain as my elbow caught a jutting rock. The pain shot through me like an electric shock. I have never understood why the point of the elbow is called the funny bone. There is nothing funny about hitting it. I almost howled in agony, but managed to confine myself to a brief but bitter profanity. Then I got up and moved onwards, slightly more slowly.

I got back to Magda and was surprised I had been gone less than ten minutes. Surprised and delighted. I didn't know how far behind us our stalker was, but a pound to a penny said he wasn't loitering. He would be moving as fast as he reasonably could.

"You okay?"

"Yes," she whispered.

I dropped to the ground and began to slither forward, sticking to the forest side of the path. About thirty metres from the position I assumed that Inspector Rodriguez had taken up, I stopped. Thirty metres. On good ground in bright light, about five seconds of hard sprinting separated us. In this light, on this ground, still under half a minute. If you didn't mind your shins taking a beating. This was the killing ground. And I was ready.

I slid my gun from my pocket and thumbed the safety off. Five bullets left in the chamber. How many would be there when this was over?

TWENTY-FOUR

I was aware of the silence. Plenty of it. It surrounded me like a security blanket. The problem with silence is that it is soothing. I was lying prone on the ground, late at night. Nothing was happening. The mind goes into autopilot, and the next thing you know, you are jerking awake and someone has a blade at your throat. That's why sentries patrol rather than sit in their boxes. You have to fight to stay awake. Tiredness isn't what puts you to sleep. It's inertia.

I've known a few snipers. They tell stories about lying under cover for days, pissing into bottles, or in some cases just pissing, immobile, and lying in their own mess. Nothing but their breathing and their heartbeat to keep them company. And they stay awake. They are a special breed of people. Not a nice breed, just special. I am not a sniper. I knew I was beginning to drift off. If I closed my eyes for a moment, I would be gone.

I tried my mindfulness training. I scanned my body for tensions, letting my attention wander from the top of my head down towards my toes. As my attention reached my chest, my eyes blinked closed for a moment and I was almost gone, but I jerked awake. Not a good strategy.

I focused on what few sounds I could hear. I strained my ears. Nothing. Not even the murmur of a breeze through the leaves. Then I faintly caught something. A cricket? Yes, a cricket. The distinctive clicking.

I greeted the sound with delight, and tried to hone in on where it was coming from. As I tuned in, I became aware of other insect noises. They were low, almost below the level of awareness. But once you found one, you found the others. A whole world was opening up to me. This was good. This would keep me awake.

When it came, it seemed to me like a boom of thunder. Objectively it was nothing like that. It was a tiny sound, and in the distance. But it was not made by an insect, and it crashed into my consciousness. A twig breaking. Someone had stood on a twig. The sound shot through my eardrum and bounced around my head.

He was coming. It was on.

I wanted to hiss a warning to Rodriguez, but I knew I could not. I had to remain in total silence. So did he. I just hoped he was still awake. I had almost succumbed, and I am used to this sort of manhunting. Was he?

My senses were in hyper-alert mode now. I made myself so still I could hear the blood pulsing through the artery in my ear. The world was silent. Eerily quiet. After the crack of the twig, there hadn't been a sound. But then I heard rustling. He was moving again.

I permitted myself a tiny smile. He had bought the ruse of the campfire. He believed we were almost half a kilometre up the trail. And if he thought that, he would throw caution to the wind and move faster, because he had to get the job done before help arrived.

I heard a bird squawk and fly up into the air. The sound was closer than the twig. In my head I reckoned he would pass Rodriguez in two or three minutes. I began counting off the seconds.

Ten seconds passed. Twenty. Thirty. A minute ticked by. Still I counted in my head. One more minute. Still nothing. It must be now. It had to be.

My breathing almost stopped as I concentrated. I could feel my leg muscles tense, ready for the explosion of power that would propel me to my feet as soon as he was in range. My fingers gripped the soil, ready to push my body into an upright position. I could feel the cold metal of the gun in my hand. I was like Usain Bolt about to start a relay, only the baton was deadly.

Another full minute passed. Nothing. Not even a noise from the woods. No bird, no rustle, no twig moving. Deathly silence. I prayed Rodriguez would not snap awake at the wrong time and betray his position. He had to be alert behind his cover, watching the approach and the passage of our assassin. The plan depended on that.

Another minute passed in agonising silence. Christ, what was happening up that path?

Now. It had to be now.

It wasn't.

Another minute — a full minute — passed. I counted it out.

Had I made a mistake? Perhaps he was not coming up the path. It might have been a fox or a feral dog. I began to relax. I didn't stand down. I just went from code red to code orange. At least now I was fully awake. That was something.

Then it kicked off.

It began with a roar.

"Deten, tu bastardo!"

I don't actually speak Spanish, but context is everything. *Stop, you bastard.* And I knew the voice. Rodriguez's. He was ignoring our plan. The plan had been simple. I would wait until the gunman was almost on me and spring up. Then Rodriguez would jump him from behind. A pincer movement. Failproof.

But Rodriguez had found a way to make it fail.

I sprang up. Cover was of no importance anymore. Speed was. But there was nothing I could do. It unfolded with the inevitability of a piece of toast falling towards the ground butter-side down. You could see it happen, you knew how it would end, your body strained to change the outcome, and the toast still buttered the lino.

I ran. My thighs pumped and my stride lengthened. I tripped, picked myself up, kept running. It was no good. I was always going to be too late.

I watched in horror as two figures emerged from the trees and grappled, moving closer and closer to the edge of the ridge. Then one of the figures disappeared over the side.

A scream pierced the air. It was long and protracted. Then there was a thud, and the scream died instantly.

The figure who had not gone over the edge turned and faced me.

Rodriguez? It looked like Rodriguez.

Shit situation, but a win is a win. Our stalker had gone over the side of the hill. He might have survived the fall, but the sudden termination of the scream did not bode well for him. He was injured or dead. He was going nowhere. I was collecting a bounty. *Yippee for me.*

I smiled as I drew to a stop and looked at him.

I stopped smiling when he raised his arm and fired at me.

The muzzle flash lit the night, and the noise filled my ears. I didn't think. My instincts took over the nano-second his hand began to rise. My left knee bent and I dropped to my side, collapsing to the ground. The first bullet passed harmlessly over my right shoulder. I went down so fast that to Rodriguez it must have looked like he had hit me.

Rodriguez? No — that made no sense. It was Rodriguez who had gone over the side.

The guy who was firing at me was our stalker. He had brought down the inspector. He was on the verge of bringing me down. Yippee my arse. That bounty was still out of reach.

From the ground I watched as he assumed a shooter's stance. I rolled. He shot. The second shot came a lot closer than the first. I continued the roll until I was up on one knee, my gun in my hand. I didn't waste time bringing my arm up. I shot from the hip.

My wrist felt the jolt, but it was a small one. A low-powered pistol, and I was used to the recoil. Shooting from the hip you lose accuracy. But a pistol is not accurate to begin with, and I was shooting in the dark. So the gain in speed made up for the fact that I wasn't going to hit him, no matter how much care I took over my aim.

I didn't disappoint myself. My shot hit nothing. But that wasn't the point. The point was that now he was under fire, and he would stop shooting at me.

He had taken two shots almost without aiming, and I returned one shot. He turned and ran, back up the path the way we had come. Back towards the nunnery and our original camp. I chased him until my foot crashed into the stream once more. The cold water drew me up, and I stopped. I could hear him crashing through the undergrowth up ahead.

Follow him or not? In its favour, it is easier to shoot at the back of a retreating man than for that man to point over his shoulder and fire blind. Against, it was dark. And he could suddenly stop and turn and put one into my chest before I knew what was happening.

Also, I was running low on ammo. Odds were he was not. So I took the sensible approach and let him go. Perhaps the cardinal would stop him with a spray of holy water.

I walked over to the edge of the ridge and looked down. I could see the damaged vegetation where Rodriguez had gone over. But the ground got steeper very quickly, and he had plunged some distance. He might have become tangled in branches, or he might have fallen a vast distance and been smashed on rocks below. Even if his fall was arrested by a tree, there was no guarantee he wasn't impaled on a broken branch, a human shish kebab.

I got as close to the edge as I could, and peered over. I could make out nothing. I strained my eyes in the darkness, and after a few moments I made out a blob of light in the darker surroundings. Straining my eyes, I was almost sure it was a rucksack. Rodriguez had been carrying a rucksack. It was a good distance down. Given time I could have climbed the slope, but not until dawn. In this light it would have been suicide.

I straightened up. Could this get any worse?

Just then, a hand grasped me firmly on the shoulder from behind and my beating heart began to breakdance.

TWENTY-FIVE

I jumped. The contents of my intestine didn't. I nearly had an embarrassing accident.

I spun rapidly. One hand came up across my body, ready to fend off a blow or deflect a gun or a knife. The other began snaking forward to throw a rapid punch.

But I pulled it.

Magda was looking at me. She flinched as she saw my fist.

"Sorry," I said. "You scared me. Why have you broken cover?"

She ignored my question. "What happened?" she said. "Where is Victor?"

Victor? It took me a moment. Then I remembered, that was his name.

"The inspector has met with a bit of an accident." I could feel her begin to crumple, and I put a hand on her shoulder. She had to hold it together.

"Is he alright?" she whispered.

How to answer? First off, I didn't actually know. He could be unconscious and might wake up in a moment, bruised and battered but unbowed. Or he might be dead, smashed to pieces on the rocks hundreds of feet below us. Not only didn't I know, I had no way of finding out. So I couldn't answer her question.

"I am sure he will be," I said. Then I hesitated. "Actually, I am not sure at all. I have no idea how he is. He went over the edge and I can hear no movement down below." I looked at her, holding her shoulder firmly. "He may be dead. He is certainly beyond our help at the moment. So we move on and get out of danger fast." I tried to turn her, but she resisted.

"What happened?" she said. "I'm not moving until you tell me."

So I told her. Normally I am a gentleman and try to spare feelings, but not in this case. The inspector had screwed up, and I let him take the blunt.

"Our plan was that Rodriguez would wait until whoever was following us passed him. Then he would come out quietly and get behind him. I would come out from my spot, and we would have the guy in a trap. But for some reason I don't understand, the inspector thought he knew better. He just jumped the guy. It all happened too fast for me to do anything. One minute they were wrestling, the next minute one went over the cliff. I thought it was our shooter, but it wasn't. It was Rodriguez. By the time I got close enough to find out, the guy started shooting at me."

"I heard the shots," she confirmed. "That's why I came out."

I sighed. "Rule of thumb for when shots ring out. You get the fuck out of Dodge. You certainly don't run towards the shots."

"You do."

"It's my job. What would you have done if he had shot me as well as sending the inspector over the edge?"

That silenced her for a moment, but somehow I didn't believe she would learn anything. Next time she would blunder blindly into danger again.

"Let's go," I said.

"Not without checking if he is still alive." She walked to the edge of the drop and grabbed a branch, leaning out. "Victor," she shouted. There was a hint of hysteria in her voice. She shouted again. Not a whimper disturbed the silence. "We'll have go to down," she said.

"Okay, we can spare a few minutes," I said, trying to keep the sarcasm out of my voice. "If you can just tie the rope to that tree trunk over there, I can lower myself down and see."

"What rope?" she asked. "I don't have any rope."

"Neither do I. That's why we move on. That, and there's a man with a gun back along the trail, and he might still be looking for us."

"We can't just leave him."

"We're not. The others will have phoned the police by this stage. In an hour, this hill will be crawling in uniforms. They can get a helicopter and lower someone down. The best thing we can do for him is to draw the shooter away, by moving on."

I could sense her reluctance.

"I think I can see something down there," she whispered.

"Yes. He had the rucksack with him. Damn fool lost our gear. I did wonder if I could get down to that ledge and retrieve it, but it would take too long and would be too dangerous in this light. We'll have to leave it." I straightened and turned.

"I do believe you are more upset about the rucksack than about Victor," she snapped.

Damn straight, I nearly snapped back. But I stopped myself. I hadn't warmed to the inspector, but I had nothing against him. And he could be leaving a family behind. I felt a bit churlish.

"Of course I am upset about him," I said. "But I am also upset that I have only three bullets left, and he took a perfectly good automatic, full magazine, over the cliff with him. There is nothing I can do for him. But if I had that gun now, it would make protecting you a lot easier. So yes, on many levels I am upset. But none of that matters now. What matters is getting you to safety. Quickly."

That seemed to get through to her, and she finally turned from the brink. "What do we do?" she asked.

"We jog."

TWENTY-SIX

We moved quickly, not caring what noise we made. I wanted to get to the campfire fast to build it up and keep it burning. Why? I was not sure. Some instinct drove me. We were on the side of a hill. We could have gone back, forward, or up. Back brought us into the line of fire if our stalker had not given up. Forward brought us away from him, but in a predictable pattern he could follow. Up the hill made a certain sense. If we were careful for the first twenty metres and didn't disturb the vegetation, there was no way he could find us. Not even with night vision goggles. To decide on our course, I put myself in his head, just as I knew he would be trying to put himself in my head. How would he see my thought process?

He would assume I had run to lay a trap for him, because he had walked into a trap. *Correct.* So he would assume I was not just a bodyguard, but a tactically aware opponent who was actively trying to catch him. *Correct.* So I would not give up. *Correct.* So the hill was out. *Correct.* Would I come after him, or run from him in the hope of drawing him onwards? That was a toss-up. But he would probably bet on my going forward. And the campfire was the logical place for me to aim for.

He would not be stupid enough to think I was going to make a stand there. Rodriguez might have made that rookie mistake, but not me. He would assume I would make it look like a camp, but then get uphill of it, and wait for him to walk in.

So much for him reasoning my thought processes. Now I would have to reason his. He would move towards the campfire. But about 200 metres short, he would make noise so that we were in no doubt that he was coming. Then he would cut off the trail, gain as much height as he could, and try to drop down on us from above, catching us by surprise. I hoped so, at least. The plan that was forming loosely in my head depended on my reading this situation correctly. No mistakes.

We got to the campfire and Magda flopped down.

"He's not going to follow us," she declared confidently. "He will know someone called the cops. He will be running away as fast as he can."

"What if he runs towards us, to get away?" I said. "It makes sense. Back towards the nunnery and the Camino, he is running into the cops. So he might come after us. And he has the rifle — don't forget that."

Her face went pale in the flickering light of the fire, and she stood and retreated to the edge of the trees. Good. She was taking this threat seriously.

I moved fast, throwing more logs on the fire and some kindling. The kindling was needed because it would burn fast, creating flames that could be seen from a distance. The logs would keep burning after we got into hiding.

Once I was satisfied with the conflagration — and I am no boy scout, so I wasn't fussy — I moved to the next part of my devious trap. I ran to the edge of the trees and yanked two shrubs out of the earth. Neither was ideal, but it was dark. I put both branches down in front of the fire as upright as I could. Then I took off my T-shirt and draped it over one of them. I hissed at Magda.

"Your T-shirt. Fast."

I could see the confusion on her face. She didn't know what I was doing, but she still trusted me. She peeled off her T-shirt and tossed it to me. That left her in a black sports bra.

"Do you always sleep in a bra?" I asked.

It was partly to keep her talking so that panic didn't return. But it was also curiosity. I know women. My sister is one. I have slept with many, and been in relationships with a few. I know that bras are not normally worn in bed. And Magda had been woken suddenly and didn't have time to make sophisticated wardrobe choices.

"These puppies are my golden ticket. I can't have them getting crushed or flopping around like some feckless hippy," she said. "You look after the tools of your trade, don't you?"

I wished Rodriguez had felt the same about his guns. But I said nothing. I placed her T-shirt over the other shrub.

"What now?" she said. "We wait until he attacks those dummies and then we jump him?"

I wished it was that easy. Those dummies wouldn't fool him for a moment.

"No. The plan is a bit more sophisticated. You go further up the trail and turn in towards the cliff. Get down low, off the path, and just wait it out until dawn. If you hear shots, don't move. If you see a bear, don't move. You only move if you hear my voice, or if the cops come. Understand?"

She nodded. "And you?"

"I am going up the hill to lay the real trap."

TWENTY-SEVEN

Credit the mindfulness training. I didn't spare a single thought for Magda once I turned from her and heard her walking off down the path. Either that, or I am a callous jerk. I trusted she would finally get the message and stay under cover. Her life depended on it.

I carefully made my way into the forest uphill of the campfire, being very careful to leave no trace. I was moving fast but cautiously at the same time. The schizophrenia of the professional assassin. I got to a spot about fifteen metres in, and perhaps six or seven metres above the campfire. The slope was steep, and I had a bird's eye view looking down.

The spot I chose was ideal. The ground levelled for a short space, and a natural break in the foliage created a sort of path down to the fire. Not an actual path. This wasn't a trail beaten flat by animals. Just a break in the vegetation, where you could force your way through a little easier than in any other spot. If you were a hiker coming down the hill and trying to find the main path, it would be the route you would instinctively try first. Nothing more. But that was all I was looking for.

That, and one other key factor.

There was a large sycamore tree that dominated the forest in that spot. The ground under the tree was a little bare because of the shadow the foliage created. I could climb the tree without breaking twigs or leaving any trace, and once I got into the lower branches I could climb out and find perfect cover. I could observe the campfire and the approaches to it — including the forest itself — in perfect concealment. I could not have conceived a better ambush spot.

My next task was to MacGyver the hell out of the terrain. Not rebooted MacGyver (why do they have to remake all the classic TV programmes?), but old-school MacGyver.

If you are not familiar with MacGyver, shame on you. You have obviously been out enjoying yourself and living when you should have been catching up on 80s television. He was an ex-army odd-jobs man who kept finding himself tangled with international gangs and killers. In every episode, he would use whatever bits and pieces were lying around to improvise traps and weapons. He could turn an old water bottle into a bazooka, a wire coat hanger into a pocket calculator, and a microwave into a ticking bomb. That one I could do myself. Just put a jam-jar of petrol in the microwave with a bit of tinfoil or a spoon in it, and put it on a timer. After a few seconds, the petrol begins to heat up and vaporise. Then the sparks from the foil or spoon ignite it, blowing up the kitchen in a satisfying sooty fireball. Handy, perhaps, when you don't want to do all the paperwork for a divorce.

I didn't have a microwave with me, and besides, there was no power this far from a socket. So my trap would not involve blowing up our stalker.

Who was our stalker? To be honest, I hadn't given that much thought. He could be anyone — literally. Profilers will pretend they can look at a modus operandi and deduce the personality of the killer. *He is a left-handed introvert who smokes a pipe.* The truth is, you can only offer vague generalisations. He was almost certainly male, because statistically these killers generally are. And more likely white than Black, for two reasons. There are more whites than Blacks in this part of Europe, and whites are statistically more often serial killers. Also, he was probably right-handed. Nothing to do with detective work there. Most of us are.

See? Profiling is a waste of time. I knew he wasn't me, Fermin, Rodriguez or Mack, because we were all at the camp together when it came under fire from outside. Knowing that left a lot of people in Spain unaccounted for.

Rodriguez believed that Magda's stalker was a real danger, and I went along with that. Stalkers sometimes cross the line from obsessive devotion to violence. And focusing on him gave me a stick to beat the inspector with once he had let the guy escape. But he was about as likely as the cardinal, if I was honest. He was stalking Magda, not the Camino. Once this was all over, I would seek him out and have a word with him. Just to finish off the protection detail of my brief. But that was a job for a different day.

I stopped thinking about it. This wasn't going to help. Instead, I went through my resources with MacGyver in mind. Unfortunately, I was not as well-resourced as the television scriptwriters generally left him. There was no wire coat hanger, no oil cans and hinges, no spare tyres, no roll of duct tape in my back pocket. I went through everything I had. It was a pitifully slim collection. I had laces on my boots, a gun, a knife, and fabric from my clothes. And branches, lots of branches. But breaking a branch made noise. So really I had no branches.

There was only one trap that would work. Carefully, I took off both my laces. They were bootlaces, so I had about six metres of strong twine if I tied them together. I tied one end to a small tree, then ran the laces tight across another tree and around it one half turn. Then I ran it into a bush and tied it off for the moment. It would act as a tripwire across the path.

The next bit I balked at, but in the end I could see no way around it. I took my gun out of my pocket and secured it in a crock of a tree, pointing just ahead of the tripwire. The barrel was aimed right at where someone would fall if they ran over the wire in a hurry. They would sprawl face first in the dirt and the gun would be aimed straight between their shoulders, assuming a height of between 165 and 185 centimetres, or five-foot-eight to six-two in old money. Don't bother checking those conversions, because I didn't. Unless our stalker was an extra from a local production of *Snow White*, the gun was going to do serious damage to him.

When I was satisfied that it was secure, I untied the end of the lace and looped it through the trigger guard and around the trigger. Most guns take a lot more pressure to fire than you would imagine. Not Rodriguez's throw-down. It was a useless heap of junk, and the trigger was loose. It was perfect for my purposes. I adjusted the tension on the tripwire and felt a small glow of satisfaction. Eat your heart out, MacGyver. This was perfect. The stalker would come down the hill, follow the natural line of least resistance, and trip over the lace. That would bring him crashing to the ground face first, and the little gun would cough it's pathetic song. Game over.

Unless he didn't follow the faint path. It was dark, and you could never tell.

I had a few minutes. So I took out my knife and used it to rip out a strip from my pants. I would have preferred to use my shirt, but it was down at the campfire, draped around a branch masquerading as me. I impaled the fabric on a branch around chest height, just to make sure he knew I had come through this way ahead of him. Even in the poor light, he couldn't miss the flash of fabric. I couldn't have made the trail any more obvious if I had painted it with glow-in-the-dark snot-green arrows. Obvious, yet not so obvious that he might smell a rat. In a word, perfect.

Now all I had to do was get into position and wait.

TWENTY-EIGHT

I waited. And waited.

It took twenty-three minutes, which was a lot longer than I expected. I counted out the minutes in my head, poised and ready. I am not sure how accurate my count was, but my internal clock rarely lets me down. At twenty minutes I thought I heard something, but strained my ears and decided I was wrong. Then at twenty-three minutes, there was no doubt. He was behind me and coming down the hill. He was moving quietly. I didn't think he could spot me. My cover was good. But I didn't know what equipment he was using, so I couldn't be sure. He could be watching me in technicolour as he came down the hill if he had access to some of the gear I occasionally get from friends in the CIA and from other sources. Or he could be stumbling in the dark. I wasn't going to risk moving just to get eyes on him.

It is one of the most stressful things, to wait in stillness with your back to a man with a gun. You feel ridiculously exposed, no matter how good your position is. You trust your training, but still you wait in anticipation of the punch of a bullet into your back. It's a weird sensation, being shot. It's different each time. Sometimes the pain is searing. Other times it is the dull ache of a heavy punch, then you feel your breath shortening and your brow beginning to seep sweat. Then you know it's a bad one.

Worst of all, I imagine, is the one you don't feel. The one that kills you instantly, taking you out of the game for the final time. I could feel my chest tightening, and I forced myself to continue breathing. I needed to be sharp. If I got the chance, I needed to be able to react instantly. If I got the chance…

Three minutes.

One hundred and eighty seconds.

I counted them in my head. Then another ten. Then…

Then, with startling suddenness, he was there. From my vantage point, I could see him moving skilfully through the foliage, barely making a noise. He was surprisingly good. He was tall and slim, and looked like a jungle veteran. He was even wearing camo fatigues. Another wannabe Rambo. His shoulders were still, but his head was moving, swaying gently to take in everything, scanning the ground ahead and around. He reminded me of one of those nodding, bobbing executive toys some people put on the dashboards of their cars.

And he reminded me of something else. When his head spun to his left, he was looking directly at my position.

It was Trevor Fleischmann — Magda's stalker!

That was a surprise. He was the last person I expected here. Was I wrong? Was he the Camino Killer? No. That would be too easy. The only explanation that made sense was that her stalker had tipped over the edge and become fully deranged. But I would sort him out tonight, once and for all.

Of course, that still left me with a serial killer to track down. Tonight had been a waste of time on that score.

I almost relaxed. I had tackled him once before, and I knew I could tackle him again. But he had gone up the hill and dropped down on the campfire rather than just blundering up the trail. So he had some tactical awareness. And he was holding a kick-ass assault rifle.

It looked like an AK47 to me, the most popular assault rifle among terrorists, rebels, and paramilitaries. It was an automatic rifle (hence the A) invented by Mikhail Kalashnikov (the K) in

1947 (the 47). The gas produced by the bullet shoots through a piston at the top of the barrel, loading the next round. In full flow, the rifle can fire 600 rounds a minute, and is accurate to around 300 metres. Not a sniper rifle, which is why he had not killed any of us back at our campsite in the nunnery. But a great all-round weapon. It has few moving parts, and never breaks down. So I knew there would be no misfire when I tackled him.

AK47s are easy to come by. There are over 75 million of them worldwide. You can buy one on the darknet for around $2,800. In the hills of Afghanistan, they change hands for around $600. And just south of the US border with Mexico, the cartels will sell you a good imitation for around $145, last time I checked. No identity check or anything.

Fleischmann probably got his in the former Yugoslavia, where there are loads of them floating around after a decade of ethnic cleansing and civil wars.

That didn't matter. What did matter was keeping out of its way. A sniper rifle will send a shockwave through your body that will kill you instantly no matter where you are hit. Take it in the shoulder, the hip, or right in the centre of your chest, and the shockwave will blitz your organs in an instant. The AK47 does not have that power. The bullets tend to go straight through. But a direct shot to the chest or head would leave me with a very serious case of death. We were playing a high-stakes game.

I watched, hardly daring to breathe, as Fleischmann crossed my line of vision. He was now slightly in front of me, and I no longer feared a bullet in the back. But I couldn't jump him, not yet. By the time I got out of cover, he would have ample opportunity to turn and fire. And he wouldn't fire a single shot. It would be a burst.

He was moving steadily forward, then he stopped. He straightened slightly and began to scan the surrounding ground. He turned.

Shit! He was staring straight at me.

TWENTY-NINE

It took all my willpower not to move. Movement now would be suicidal. I didn't have time to tackle him before he could get a shot off. His eyes seemed to bore straight into my face. Then he turned and continued scanning the forest.

He had missed me.

I whispered a thanks to the Gods of War that I had taken a moment to smear damp earth on my face, dulling my complexion.

He looked forward and took one step. He was following the layout of the land, and was heading right where I needed him to go. Just a few steps more now and he would be at the subtle opening in the vegetation.

But he was moving too slowly. He needed to be moving at a normal pace to trip over the wire. If he hit the wire at this snail's pace, he might not even move it enough to engage the trigger of the concealed gun. And he certainly wouldn't trip, so the bullet would punch into the ground and miss him by a country mile.

There wasn't anything I could do. It wasn't as if he was a dog I could shoo along the trail. If I moved, if I so much as made a noise, he would spin and find me. If he stayed moving cautiously, he would hit it but not fall, and not get shot. Only if he began to move at a more normal pace would my trap work. And he was showing no signs of speeding up. In fact, he had been slow all night. He was a lot more cautious than most hunters. It almost felt like he was the prey.

I willed him forward, but mental telepathy is a hippy fantasy and I knew he was not picking up my 'vibes'. I just had to wait this one out and play whatever hand I was dealt in the next few moments.

I watched as he edged his way closer to the gap. Another few steps. But he was still moving far too slowly. More worryingly, he was scanning the ground like a bloodhound on the scent. He stopped for a moment as his eyes caught the ragged piece of cloth dangling from a branch, and he straightened as he pulled it off and looked at it closely. He turned slowly, looking at the path he had come down, at the big tree overlooking the scene, at the pathway ahead, faint and forbidding. I almost thought I saw him smile in the pale light, but that was more likely my fevered imagination.

Then he bent down. I thought he would stand and walk on, but instead he looked for all the world like an entomologist checking out the hedgerows for a new species of beetle. His head swivelled in his characteristic motion. Then he dropped to one knee and his hand stretched out.

He had found my shoelace.

His finger ran delicately along it's line, finding the tree it was tied to. Then he began following it the other way, around the small tree, into the foliage. He couldn't miss it. A blind hunter couldn't fail to find it.

He stepped to the side of the bush and fumbled for a moment, then straightened up with Rodriguez's throw-down gun in his hand. This time, I knew his face wore a look of triumph. He had evaded my trap. When he looked around now, it was not with the look of a man carefully choosing his steps, but with the look of a conqueror.

He was sure of his ground. His shoulders were straighter and he seemed to have grown a few inches. All in my head, of course.

It didn't take him long to locate my tree. He grunted in triumph.

I knew what was going through his head. He knew I could see him. But he also knew he had the superior firepower. He had not been surprised that I had a gun, because I had fired at him when he had thrown Rodriguez over the edge. That must have caught him off-guard. No one walks the Camino armed. But now he knew about the gun. And now he had the gun in his hand. He stuffed it into his pocket, and looked deep into the canopy of the tree. His eyes scanned the foliage, looking for any clue as to my location.

I didn't move. He was right. I didn't have a second gun. No one walks the Camino armed.

Now he was directly under the tree, looking up.

And now I triggered the next phase of my MacGyver trap. I swung my arm quickly and a rock flew through the air. I pride myself on a good aim, and the distance was not great. The rock hit its target high up in the tree. The target was dislodged from a fork in the foliage. It began tumbling through the air, down towards the man waiting below. Fleischmann looked up, and a startled expression crossed his face. Then his hands came up to protect him as a wasps' nest crashed out of the sky and landed in his face.

I would love to report the angry howl of thousands and thousands of angry insects. But the wasps' nest was long abandoned. If it had not been, there is no way I could have plied it from its position in a rotten trunk and balanced it on a branch three metres overhead.

But he didn't know that. When a wasps' nest falls on your head, you drop everything in your hands and you beat the air frantically to protect your face. You dance like you have taken a shot of mains voltage to your testicles. You panic.

Fleischmann did none of that. He swatted the hive away with one hand, and brought the AK47 up with his other hand. The hive bounced harmlessly off the ground, and broke into two. Dead wasps spilled out.

Fleischmann looked straight up at where the hive had fallen from. He brought his second hand up to the gun, and steadied it. I looked at the magazine. The thought process went on almost subconsciously. Regular magazine; takes thirty rounds. He had fired two at me at our ambush site, and another three at the nunnery site. That left 25 rounds. Two and a half seconds on full automatic. He was about to light up the tree like it was Christmas. Looking at his face, I could see the fury and venom there. And the triumph.

His finger tightened on the trigger…

THIRTY

But he had screwed up. I wasn't in the tree. That was my trap. The tree was the only logical place to hide, so I had not hidden there. But I had made it look like I was there. That was the purpose of the tripwire. I never expected him to miss the lace across the path. He was meant to find it. And to make sure, I had left a strip of fabric at eye level. He had fallen for it. The fabric put him on alert, and he found the lace tripwire and the crude trap just like I wanted him to. Then he had looked around and found the only spot I could have been hidden.

That was his big mistake. I was actually under a fallen tree trunk, rotten to the core. The trunk I had found the dead wasp's nest in. I was prone on the ground, my face in the mud. Spiders crawled over my skin and maggots were in my hair. All sorts of things I didn't want to think about had crawled into my clothing, and I could feel the unpleasant tickling sensations all over my body. And something had bitten me. More than once. In short, it was disgusting. But it was deep cover. All I had to do was slither out from under the trunk, toss off the branches and leaves that covered me, scramble over some thick vegetation, and tackle Fleischmann from behind.

Four seconds, if I was hopelessly optimistic. A more realistic estimate was six to eight seconds. The plan could have worked if he had dropped his AK47 when the wasps' nest had hit him.

He hadn't.

He was looking up at the tree, waiting for me to betray my position.

"I can see you," he sang out. "Come down and I will kill you clean and fast."

I didn't move. Neither did anyone else up in the tree.

Seconds ticked by in agonising elongation. Every one felt like an eternity. I could hear my heart beating — and feel something crawling across my cheek towards my nose and upper lip.

He broke before I did. He fired a single burst — three shots. Torn leaves rained down on him. A small animal scurried away.

"You're good," he said. "But this only ends one way. You die. Come down and I'll make it fast. Stay up there, and I will burn you out. That will be fun."

Another minute passed, and he brought the gun up again. Perhaps by now he was having some doubts, but where else could I be? He sighted along the barrel.

I stood.

He spun. I was upright, but still in the vegetation. Four metres separated us. I held my hands up.

"We'll come out," I said. I looked back over my shoulder and made a gesture with my hand, then stepped clear of the undergrowth, and onto the clear ground under the tree. I took a half-step forward.

"That's enough."

No, it wasn't. Two metres still separated us. At least. And the gun was aimed unwaveringly at my chest.

"Come out, Magda," I called. If he bought it, the bluff would buy me time. I stood straight and faced him. "Why?" I asked.

He grinned. "Is this where I spill out my guts to you? Are you looking for closure?"

"No, mate," I grinned back. "I'm just mildly curious. I just have one question really. Is this about Magda, or is she incidental?"

A strange light came into his eyes. "Wouldn't you like to know!" Then he sensed he was being drawn down the rabbit hole of distraction. "Come out, Magda," he bellowed. He looked beyond me into the trees.

A little over two metres to cover. Say two and a half. With a gun pointed right at my chest, his finger on the trigger.

I remembered a day six years earlier. A long day. My dojo had a guest instructor from Japan. An elderly man, but the toughest bastard I had ever trained with. For four hours, he had put us through the wringer. Press-ups, burpees, squats, stomach crunches. Wind sprints, then loops of the football field beside the hall. Then do it all again. At the end of the four hours, we were broken. Standing seemed to be a major athletic achievement. That was when the training actually began.

His theory was that technique deserts you when you are exhausted, and fighting is exhausting work. So he had pushed us to the brink, then began drilling techniques.

I wasn't exhausted now, but I knew I could execute the technique flawlessly. The problem was, it was a bizarre technique, that I assumed would never be of any practical use. Was now the occasion to prove me wrong?

I opened my mouth to say something more, but he jerked the gun in my direction. He wasn't having it. I would have to produce Magda swiftly, or he would just shoot me and go for her himself.

So it was now or never. I was resigned. I had lived a fun life and would leave a beautiful(ish) corpse. If I went for it, I might live. Or I might not. But if I didn't go for it, I certainly wouldn't survive the next few minutes.

I didn't rush him. Instead, I dropped my arms to shoulder height, holding them out in front of me. Then I bent my knees, dropped my head, and threw myself towards him in a forward roll. The palms of my hands met the ground, then I tucked my head to my chest and my body rolled on. The back of my head made contact with the ground first, then my neck, then my back. My momentum carried me forward in a tight tuck. The ground spun and then the tumble was complete. I came to rest on my feet, still tucked low.

The thing about a human body tucked for a roll is that you are considerably lower than someone standing. If you tuck tight enough, you barely reach the height of someone's thighs. My head was on the level of his hips, and I was staring at his crotch from below. More importantly, the roll had closed the two-metre gap between us. I was now within grabbing distance of Fleischmann.

Of course, he hadn't been just standing there when I dropped below his sight line and began rolling. Instinctively his finger had tightened on the trigger, and he had fired a burst at where I had been standing. But the rounds had passed harmlessly over my head.

He grasped the new situation quickly, and lowered the barrel of the gun to get me back in sight. But I was too close to him, and the stock of the gun came down over my shoulder. The gun was too long to be used effectively at such close quarters.

I had all the time in the world, and I savoured the moment. I reached out and grasped both his ankles with my hands. Then I stood suddenly and jerked upwards. His feet came off the ground and his body flipped backwards. He flew through the air and landed heavily on his back. The AK47 dropped harmlessly to the side.

Then he made another mistake.

If he had retrieved the rifle and leaned away from me, he would have had room to take the shot. Instead, he reached into his pocket and drew out Rodriguez's throw-down pistol.

"Got you," he said as he aimed it straight between my eyes. Then he pulled the trigger.

Nothing happened.

He pulled again. Same result.

I had never expected him to fall over the tripwire. I knew the booby trap would not get him. So I had removed the bullets. All three were now rattling in my pocket. I couldn't keep the smile from my face.

Time to apply the coup de grâce. I took a half-step forward with my left leg, then drew my right back. Like a footballer about to take the penalty that would win the cup, I gave the kick everything. Straight between his legs.

I felt a satisfying thunk of foot meeting yielding flesh and he grunted in pain. But he had already begun spinning as I launched the kick, and his momentum kept him going. And now my foot was caught between his thighs as he turned.

In an instant I was falling to the side, my leg trapped. I hit the ground and my head bounced off a rock. I saw stars. They literally danced in front of my eyes, before skittering away as my head cleared. Fleischmann was scrambling to his feet. I scrambled to meet him. We came together under the sycamore, and he gripped me in a wrestler's hold. It was an uneven contest. I was stronger and faster than him, and a hell of a lot better trained. And I fight dirty. I grabbed his hair and yanked down, pulling him onto his left leg. Then I kicked the leg out from under him. He crashed back to the ground. I didn't give him a chance to scramble back up. I was on him like a bad rash, pinning his chest to the ground and trying to control his arms.

But he had one last trick up his sleeve. In the struggle, he must have felt the knife dangling from my belt. Before I could stop him, he had it in his hand and he lashed out blindly. I felt a searing pain through my biceps, and I almost let go of his other arm. But giving him any leeway could be lethal now, and

I forced myself to hold on despite the pain. He swung his arm down to get room for another swipe, and I shifted my weight, then grabbed his wrist and pushed it into the ground. He was on his back with one arm pinned, and I was sitting across his chest, forcing my weight down to drive the air from his lungs. On the ground just beyond us was the stone I had thrown at the wasps' nest. I reached for it, and brought it crashing down on his hand. He screamed in pain, and dropped the knife. I lifted the stone and crashed it down a second time. I felt the bones crush under the blow, and when I brought my hand back up it was wet with blood.

I swivelled off his chest and scrambled to my feet, laying hold of his rifle. I swung the barrel down and around until it was aimed straight at him.

"It's over," I said.

THIRTY-ONE

He looked at me forlornly for a few minutes, gingerly nursing his injured hand.

"You didn't have to do that," he complained.

"No," I agreed. "I could have let you kill me."

I know the pain of a crushed hand, but I wasn't feeling the guilt. This was not down to me.

"We need to talk," I said. I still needed to know if this was about Magda or if I had just caught the Camino Killer. "Are you behind all the killings?" I asked.

"Fuck you," he said.

"Now, now! No need to take that tone. I'll call in the cavalry and get someone to give you a shot of morphine for that hand, but before I do that, you need to answer my questions. I have all night. I'm in no pain."

This was not strictly true, because my bicep was aching like a bitch. I hate knife fights. There are never good outcomes. But in his own pain he had probably forgotten he had inflicted damage on me.

"Let's take it from the top," I tried again. "But let's try a different approach. Tell me, how long have you been a fan of Magda?"

He looked at me in cold fury, then suddenly stood and turned from me. I clicked the safety off.

"Do it," he bellowed. Then he began to run, crashing through the undergrowth.

I nearly did. I came so close to pulling that trigger and sending a quick burst through the back of his retreating head. A quick double tap to bring this whole ugly night to an end.

What stayed my fire was the knowledge that Fermin had almost certainly called in the rescue. Cops would be swarming this hill well before dawn, and I would have to explain a man shot in the back. If he had died in our struggle, I could have got away with it. If I had caught him on a different night, with no cops expected, I could have taken my time and disposed of the body. But my hands were tied. I could not shoot him in the back.

I chased after him. This time, the irony registered. He charged straight down the narrow gap in the vegetation where I had put my booby trap. Now he was not taking his time. He was in a blind dash, and had the tripwire still been there, he would have crashed to the ground. The gun might even have fired on an empty chamber.

I followed. I moved as fast as I dared. I was not going to risk a fall in the darkness. But I was not going to let him get too far ahead either. He cleared the edge of the forest and jumped the ditch. Nothing had tripped him, so I took a chance and leapt the ditch too, hardly slowing my run. He ran across the short clearing towards the campfire, and jumped right across it. I ran around it. He had gained about five metres.

Would he go right or left? Back towards the nunnery, or forward to where Magda was clinging to cover off the edge of the trail?

He did neither.

He kept running, right towards the edge of the clearing. He didn't slow. Too late, I realised he was planning to jump.

"Stop," I roared. I slowed and brought the barrel up, lining the sights. I could put a round in his thigh. With luck, I wouldn't hit the femoral artery. Even now I didn't want a corpse to explain.

But there wasn't time. He reached the edge without diminishing his speed, and he threw himself over with the abandon of an Olympic long jumper.

As he launched himself into the void he roared Magda's name, a last howl of defiance to the world. As he disappeared from view it was the last thing I heard, the elongated howl of: "Magdaaaaa…"

And then the thud from below.

THIRTY-TWO

Magda was as shocked as I was. When it was obvious to me that he was as deceased as Victor Rodriguez, I ran down the path calling Magda's name. She was about two hundred metres further on, where the fall-off was less steep. She had scrambled down a bit and wedged herself against a thick bush. I reached down and pulled her up onto the path.

"It's over," I whispered.

She looked into my face and saw it was true. She had been holding it together well, but now the danger was removed it was like someone had pulled a plug, releasing all the pent-up tension. It began with a sigh, which quickly turned to a sob. Then she was in my arms, shaking like a leaf in the breeze. I held her until the shaking subsided and the sobs petered out. Her skin felt clammy under my fingers, and cold. Realising that brought me back to our situation.

"We better get you back to the campfire and get your T-shirt back on," I said. I held her as we walked back down the trail. She wasn't there yet, but I could feel she was coming around.

At the campfire it looked so normal. You'd look at it and imagine boy scouts singing around it and telling ghost stories. Two people were sitting staring into the flames.

Actually, that part is not true. But it looked like two people. I had to admit my decoy looked good from a distance. I went up to one of the seated figures and pulled Magda's top off the bush. I handed it to her, and she pulled it on gratefully. Then I retrieved my own shirt and pulled it on. We all have our hang-ups, and mine is damaged clothing. I have always hated wearing shirts with missing buttons, trousers with holed knees, and jackets with tears. I had torn a strip from my pants earlier in the evening to draw Fleischmann into my trap. I won't go so far as to say I now regretted that, but I certainly wasn't happy. I could feel the cool night air through the hole, a constant reminder that the pants were going in the bin first thing tomorrow morning.

Now dressed, we stood by the fire.

"Who was it?" she asked quietly.

I sighed. She had to know sometime. "It was Georg Fleischmann. Your tame stalker."

She shrugged. "It was always a possibility," she admitted. "He was obsessed with me, he was crazy, and he had a history of violence."

This was news to me. She had been adamant that he was just a harmless loon. Now he had a history of violence? That would have to be gone into, but not now. Now it was too raw.

I left her and walked to the edge of the cliff, where he had thrown himself over. I could see nothing. It was just like the spot where the inspector had gone over. The darkness was too thick. The morning would unveil its secrets. I walked back and stood beside Magda.

"We should make our way back. The danger has passed, and they'll be looking for us."

I took her gently, and we began to walk back. We took our time. We walked slowly, and we didn't try to conceal our presence. There was no need. No one was chasing us now.

It was almost pleasant in the starlight. The night was still dark, and the trail was still overgrown. So progress was slow. And now that the tension had eased, we both felt the cold. We tried to keep a solid pace. We weren't talking. I don't suppose there was anything to say.

We weren't even halfway back to the nunnery campsite when we saw the lights. Bobbing and swaying in the distance, like lights on distant fishing boats. There were about three of them. Then six. They were getting closer and closer. Just an hour too late, the cavalry had arrived.

When we got close enough, I called out. Within minutes we were accosted by two uniformed cops. They carried guns, and were distinctly hostile. Then Magda smiled her golden smile, and they were like putty in her hands. By the time we got back to their command centre, at our first campsite, it was like we were old friends. Our arrival had something of the air of a triumph.

Cardinal Benoluchi ran forward and threw his arms around Magda. She returned the embrace with enthusiasm, and the last of the reserve broke down. Cheers broke out among our rescuers.

A paramedic ran over and threw a blanket over her shoulders and led her to a pop-up shelter, where he sat her on a bench and another paramedic produced a flask. I, of course, was ignored.

Fermin grinned at me. "They all fall for a pretty face." He reached across and took my hand firmly. "It is good to have you back safe, my friend."

His greeting was warm, but both of us knew we had things to discuss.

"Give me five minutes," I said.

I spent the five minutes retrieving a light jacket from my tent, changing my pants, and finding my phone. No missed calls, of course. No one rings you in the middle of the night. But some of the features would have been useful. Including the night vision app.

I went over to where the cardinal was sitting on a stump beside what had once been our campfire. As I sat, he passed over a hip flask. I sipped gratefully and felt the burn as the liquid slid down my welcoming throat. Good cognac. I won't say it wasn't needed.

"Tough night?"

I nodded my agreement. "He's dead," I said.

The cardinal blessed himself. "And…"

"Victor is dead too. Or badly injured."

I had already briefed our rescuers when we encountered them first, and they had radioed base for a team to try and retrieve him. The cardinal knew this. He blessed himself a second time.

"Victor. Funny, I always think of him as Rodriguez. Somehow he seemed too precise a man for first names. So, tell me from the beginning."

And I did. He listened carefully, occasionally asking a question. At the end, we sat in silence for a few minutes as he digested it all.

"You are certain it was Fleischmann? I don't see him fitting our profile."

That was the elephant in the room. We had baited a trap and captured prey. But was it *our* prey? If Fleischmann was not our Camino Killer, then we had done all this for nothing. Perhaps our puffing up of Magda's profile had just pushed an obsessive stalker over the edge. Had we put her life in danger for no reason?

He sighed. "I hate to ask, but I have to. Your account of how he died…"

"I didn't push him. I told you, my job was to capture him for prosecution, not hunt him down and kill him. That was the brief."

"And are you sure he killed himself? Might it not have been an accident? It is so easy to run the wrong way in the darkness."

"Fermin, I can't say what was going through his mind as he ran from me. I had a gun, and maybe he thought I was going to shoot him in the back. He certainly would have done that to me, and we judge people by our own standards. Or perhaps he finally realised that he had gone too far. This wasn't going to get him a slap on the wrist and a restraining order. This was going to get him a decade behind bars for attempted murder. Maybe he couldn't face that. But there is no doubt in the world. He ran for that cliff edge and he leapt over it like he was jumping into bed."

A pained look crossed Fermin's face. "You realise how that presents me with a difficulty? His body will be retrieved, and the recovery team will bring him here, for evacuation to the morgue. And I am a senior cleric. I will be asked to perform the last rites. It is a mortal sin to take your own life. A mortal sin that allows no atonement, because the poor man died without the chance to sincerely repent. You see the problem? I am not God. I cannot forgive him. Yet I can't send him to eternal flames."

We were silent for a moment, then I said: "It was dark there, and the slope did not look as bad as in other places. I think he was hoping that the vegetation would break his fall and that he would slide to safety."

The cardinal smiled softly, and put an arm on my shoulder. "Thank you," he said. "You are a good man."

THIRTY-THREE

Dawn was breaking. Sunrise was alive with the chorus of songbirds. Midges thickened the air. Bats flitted in the gloaming. It is a myth that they are nocturnal animals. They come out at dusk and dawn, feeding on the flying smorgasbord of insect life.

Magda was in a sleeping bag, on an airbed, her chest gently rising and falling. I was finishing my initial statement to a bored uniform. A helicopter had landed near the modern sculpture a few kilometres up the trail, waiting to evacuate the dead and the walking wounded. Magda would fly out. That was a safe bet. They loved her. I might have to walk. I don't inspire love.

Someone prepared breakfast. A slice of Spanish omelette, served cold, with a coffee so strong and thick and pungent the spoon stood in it without help. It was delicious.

I was preparing to move out and walk to the next village — all downhill, and a distance of about six kilometres — when the first of the two bodies was recovered. I could see the stretcher bearers coming along the path. There were four of them, two at the front and two at the rear. Mack perked up when he spotted them. He stood and began to rummage in his rucksack. A few minutes later he was running towards the rescuers, a tripod over his shoulder. Suddenly, his sexy travelogue had become something more exciting.

He gave me a cheeky thumbs up as he passed. "Award season, mate. This is the twist that lifts this tawdry porno into the art category."

Somehow I doubted it. True crime is a niche as tawdry as travel or made-for-TV erotica. He wasn't adding value to Magda's film, just muddying its genre. But he seemed happy, and that had to count for something.

He got his camera into position and stood behind it, adjusting the sights. He looked into the viewfinder, then crouched and watched as the stretcher-bearers approached. He tracked them, panning the camera slightly and adjusting the view for a dramatic low-angle shot. Suddenly, he stood up and shouted, "Holy shit! I'll be stuffed!"

That got my attention, and I turned towards him. He had snatched his camera off the tripod and was running towards the stretcher, shooting as he ran. He seemed excited.

I stood up and ran towards him. Something was clearly up.

As I got closer, I realised what it was; the man on the stretcher was not dead. My first clue was that his face wasn't covered. As I got closer, I could see that his face was moving, looking around. Closer still, I could see that he was talking.

Who was it? Rodriguez, or Fleischmann? If it was Fleischmann, we could complete the interrogation and find out if he was the Camino Killer. But I was rooting for Rodriguez. It wasn't even close.

So I was delighted when I got close and the policeman spotted me and his face broke into a big grin.

"My friend, did you kill him?" he called.

I shrugged. Yes and no. It didn't matter. "How are you here? We thought you were dead!" I said.

"Don't ask me. I remember going over the edge. Then I remember waking up in agony. I think my leg is broken. And I'm starving. And my head hurts like a bitch. But don't ask me beyond that. When I woke up, I began to pull myself up the hill to the path. But it wasn't easy. I had to drag my leg.

Couldn't put any weight on it. It must have taken me all night. But these kind men came along in time to haul me up the last two metres. Fine lot of good they did me. And my trousers are ruined." He laughed, and the four men carrying him laughed with him. There was an easy intimacy between them. "At least they carried me back here. And I gather there is a helicopter waiting for me."

"You seem remarkably cheerful for a man who almost died."

"What can I say? I am one of the glass-half-full people. That, and the fact that I am injected up to the eyeballs with morphine. Which I greatly recommend. I want to give the world a big hug." With that, he seemed to tune out. His eyes became sticky with dreams, and he sighed and stopped talking.

Mack said: "Positions everyone. Let's get that shot again, this time without interruptions."

But the four guys just picked up their pace and walked on. Mack followed them, doing his best to get the defining shot. I jogged back to Cardinal Benoluchi.

"Rodriguez survived. Don't ask me how, but he's on that stretcher."

He smiled. "I can't take all the credit, but I did a lot of praying last night."

"You can't take any of the credit," I laughed.

Three hours later, I was sitting in the lobby of the small hotel in Puente La Reine. I was showered, watered, and fed, and felt a lot better with the world. Benoluchi was beside me, this time dressed in black, complete with dog collar. He had his medieval silver crucifix around his neck. Beyond that, there was no sign of ostentation. No outward sign that we were in the presence of a prince of the church.

Despite the early hour, there was a bottle of red wine open in front of us. A very good bottle of wine. The aroma wafted across the room to me when I had come down from freshening up. Fermin had passed me a glass and I had not turned it down. I am not a morning drinker, but the events of the night before felt like a hard day's work and I hadn't slept. So, in some sense the morning was metaphorically the evening, and I felt entitled to a glass.

I savoured the aroma for a while, then finally tried a sip. It was rich and sweet and I could taste all sorts of undertones. Don't ask me any more. I don't know wine. But even a moron could tell this was the good stuff. So I sipped it slowly and enjoyed it. We drank in silence, looking out the window at the street. Pilgrims, eager and bright-eyed, strode past, their Nordic poles click-clacking on the concrete pavement.

"You like the wine?" the cardinal finally asked.

"I do. As my sister once said about something else, it tastes as good as God's sweat."

He raised an eyebrow.

"Yes. She was talking about... Well, she was in an experimental period of her life. Look, I'm not going to tell a cardinal what she was talking about."

He smiled. But it had set me thinking about my sister. I really needed to get her advice on my brother's holiday plans.

We were starting our second glass when Inspector Rodriguez hobbled into the room. He was using crutches to walk, and his left leg was swaddled in an inflatable emergency splint. His face was pale, he was moving slowly, and he had a strange gleam in his eye. He sat heavily and reached for an empty glass.

"Just wet it, and I'll sniff. It smells fantastic. But no tasting. Just like you must not mix the grape and the grain, you must not mix the grape and the morphine. So says my doctor."

"You're medicated?" I asked.

"Gloriously medicated. And loving it."

"How long will you be out of action?"

"A few hours, maybe a day. The morphine will be reduced as the pain comes under control. To be honest, I feel nothing. Later, I will get this temporary splint removed and the leg will be put in plaster. Maybe three months. But I will be able to get around on my crutches, so I will be back at my desk in a few days. Now that the Camino Killer is out of commission."

The cardinal raised his glass, and I raised mine. But I wasn't so sure.

"You think Fleischmann was the Camino Killer?" I asked.

Rodriguez shrugged. "I really don't know. But it is possible. I think, probable. Too much of a coincidence that he is just here for Magda. I have made a few calls. We have his home address and the German police are raiding it as we speak. That will give us a better idea."

"How soon will we know?" asked the cardinal.

"A few hours. First they need to apply for a court order. Then they need to execute it. I expect word by lunchtime."

Magda hadn't joined us. She was still fast asleep. But Amanda and Mack did make an appearance. They were excited. The action of the previous night had given them a great story. They couldn't see the bigger picture. One man was dead. Another was lucky not to be.

There was an even bigger picture. A killer was stalking the Camino and had taken four victims in four years. This might be the end of his campaign of hate and violence. I got why they did not see that big picture. No one did. As the four previous killings were all radically different, no one had connected them yet — beyond the Spanish police and the Vatican. But had he succeeded in killing Magda, then surely a fifth year with a bizarre killing on the Camino would not have gone unnoticed. I could have clued them in, but I didn't. Nor the small cluster of other journalists who had descended like locusts on the scene. Journalists constantly surprise me. It is all about the story, as if it were a work of fiction and not something that impacts flesh and blood people with real emotions and fears. I listened to them babbling on excitedly, probably already planning their awards season speeches. I let them have their morning.

Fermin and I began a game of chess. I like the game, but I don't get to play it regularly. Fermin, on the other hand, was based in a city full of celibate men, all looking for something to sublimate their frustrations. So he was a bit of a chess whizz kid. I played a standard opening, and he responded with an unorthodox defence. The game went downhill from there. I found myself defending my king with a knight and a bishop, to his queen, two knights, and a rook. It was a massacre. The second game was not much better, but I did manage to postpone my defeat a little longer this time.

You get the picture; we had a lazy morning. Inspector Rodriguez sat in a wicker chair in the sunlight and dozed gently. I believe he was still under the influence. We ordered an early lunch. I chose garlic soup of the region, thickened with stale bread. It was simple but well made, and was paired with a baguette and olive oil. I was nearly finished when the call came through. Rodriguez stood to take it, then hobbled out to the reception. He came back about ten minutes later and gestured to Fermin and me. An hour later, a helicopter picked us up from a pad behind the local fire station, and whisked us to Santander airport. A small private plane was on the runway, and we flew straight to Berlin. Just the two of us, myself and Cardinal Benoluchi.

THIRTY-FOUR

The Church has unlimited resources. That was obvious when I saw the helicopter and the plane. But it keeps those resources by being tighter than a duck's arse with expenses. The plane was a rust bucket with a strong fan out front doubling as a propeller. The noise from the engine made it sound like we were in a washing machine, and when we hit a bit of turbulence over the Pyrenees, that feeling was reinforced. Conversation was impossible, and thankfully the cardinal had left the chess board in Spain, so I was spared further humiliation.

We landed at a small airport outside Berlin, and a limo was waiting for us. It was the first chance we had to talk properly since the inspector's bombshell.

"I don't really know why I'm here," I said, again. "This is way beyond my area of expertise."

"Mine too. I am an economist and an expert in canon law. Neither of which will help me here. But you are an expert on evil. You have walked evil paths and mixed with evil people, and yet retained your humanity. I want your raw impressions on what you see. I want you to tell me whether this is over or not."

One thing I learned during my time in the army: you do not argue with the paymaster. So I went along for the ride.

I had never been to Berlin before. I have heard it is a wonderful city, full of history and character. I don't know; we were driven to a suburb that could have been the edge of any European metropolis. The only thing that distinguished it was that the houses looked a little poorer than most European suburbs, and the atmosphere a little more dowdy. I didn't need to ask. We were driving through what had once been East Berlin. It had that dour communist feel.

We ended up outside an apartment block, about six storeys high. There were four blocks surrounding a small area of open grass, which contained some parkland, a playground, and a football field. But if the apartments appeared down at heel, the cars in the street were good. Many were new, many high end.

Fermin wrinkled his nose. "In Berlin, this is a desirable neighbourhood. In Rome, we would shudder to think of living here."

It was obvious where we needed to go. Three police cruisers and two white vans were parked outside the main entrance to the building we had pulled in beside.

Benoluchi — who had opted for the full scarlet on this trip — strolled imperiously across to the officer who looked like he was in charge. The man bowed, then took the cardinal's proffered hand.

"Officially, you are not allowed to examine the scene. We are letting you look as a courtesy, but you must do nothing else. Just observe."

The cardinal nodded.

"And your friend?" The cop pointed to me.

"He is a forensic psychologist that the Vatican called in to try and profile the killer. We want him to see whether Fleischmann fits the profile."

I smiled and nodded, the way I thought an expert would behave when introduced to the cop guarding a building he wanted to enter. Sort of like I knew I belonged, and expected my credentials to be accepted without challenge. Inwardly I was cursing Benoluchi — he could have given me a head's up.

I would have come up with some bullshit to sound like a psychologist.

But my nod seemed to do the trick. A lowly uniform was summoned and told to escort us up to the apartment.

We took the lift. It stopped on the fourth floor. I said: "I am impressed with your influence."

"Germany is a very Catholic country. People forget that. But we don't. We can get doors opened."

We walked down the corridor from the elevator. We walked to the door of apartment 43. There was a yellow police tape covering the door. The cop removed the tape and opened the door, gesturing us in.

"No touching, Your Eminence," he warned. We stepped through.

The entrance door — which I noticed was steel-reinforced — led into a small living room. It was standard enough. Against one wall was a two-seater sofa, and there were two matching easy chairs. They were cream leather, which whispered money. There was a glass coffee table which was bare except for a guidebook to the Camino and a German language edition of Stephen King's *Rage*, looking old and well-thumbed.

"Interesting," I muttered.

Benoluchi looked at me blankly, so I explained.

"*Rage* is about a school shooting. It's been linked to at least five school shooting incidents in the eighties and nineties. Stephen King allowed it to go out of print, and has refused to reissue it. Seeing this on a bookshelf would ring alarm bells for anyone involved in law enforcement. And this copy is well read."

Next I looked at the television, a large flatscreen plasma job connected to a few boxes underneath. Cable, internet and

DVD would be my guesses. But I was not supposed to touch, so I didn't investigate. The television was on a corner unit, and there were about a dozen DVDs on the shelf under it. I looked at the spines. *The Greatest Showman, Evita, Riverdance, Les Misérables.* A sort of pattern was emerging here, which was broken by the next title: *Anal Dreams*.

The cop was not looking at me, so I pulled it out slightly to see the cover. Bingo — it starred Magda Lynn.

The rest of the sitting room didn't tell us much, so we moved on to the kitchenette. All this revealed was that Fleischmann was a bit of a slob, and he seemed to be vegetarian. And he preferred television meals to cooking. That last was a crime in my book, but he was beyond prosecution now.

Our next port of call was the bedroom. Here was further evidence that our man was a slob. The bed was unmade and a towel was thrown casually on the floor. Of more interest, there were four large posters — including one tacked to the ceiling. The cardinal blushed when he looked up. Not much was left to the imagination. Magda had two fingers where fingers don't normally go, and she was spreading her cheeks so that there could be no doubt about her intentions.

The other three posters were less explicit, but not by much. We were going down the rabbit hole and entering wacko country.

The bathroom revealed nothing but a male waxing kit — I didn't know such things existed. Now I do. That left one final room, the small guest bedroom.

We stood in front of it, and our eyes met. This was it. Neither of us knew what was on the other side. But we knew this was why we were here. When Rodriguez had returned to us after taking the call from Berlin, he had popped a pill, then begun talking. He liked moments of drama, and had prolonged the revelation. Too long, as it turned out … the morphine had hit before he finished his tale.

"You'll see when you get there," he had concluded, then put his head in his hands and started snoring.

So we were looking at the door, wondering what we would see inside.

"It's through that door," said the cop.

"He has a talent for stating the obvious," whispered the cardinal, with a wink. We both smiled.

Then we took a deep breath, pushed the door, and walked through.

"It's over," whispered the cardinal, after a minute's stunned silence. I had to agree.

The guest bedroom had been converted into a home office. There was a desk with a computer. On the walls were seven cork notice boards. The first was covered with pictures of the crucified banker, including a close-up in full colour that was very artistically composed and very depraved. It was strangely beautiful and stomach-crunchingly horrible at the same time. It had obviously been taken by the killer and, from the expression on the banker's face, shortly before rather than after his awful death. The eyes looked out in mute appeal, and it pained me that I could never answer that appeal.

The rest of the board was filled with smaller photos, charts, maps, and news reports. Below the board was a thick manila file stuffed with sheets.

"Newspaper clippings, photos, reports, that sort of stuff. All on the first killing," said the cop.

I scanned the other boards. Each was dedicated to a single killing, and the fifth was dedicated to Magda. I looked at it with keen interest. There was a map of hilly terrain that had some villages, but it was not of any area I recognised.

"It's about a week on from where we were last night on the walk," said the cardinal. "A rural area between Burgos and Sahagun."

"He must have planned on taking her there, but when the opportunity arose he moved early," I said. I scanned the board for any clue as to how he was going to kill her, but could find nothing. I didn't suppose it mattered anymore.

Finally, I turned to the last two notice boards. They were entirely empty.

"He had planned on continuing for another two years at least," I said.

The cop came up behind us. "There were files on the computer. Videos he took of the victims as they died. I have been authorised to show you."

I have seen a lot of hurt, pain and death. I have caused more than my fair share of it. I wasn't sure I wanted to take on any more. Benoluchi, green about the gills, was already walking out the door. He was a good man, and what he had seen today would burden him for a long time. I shook my head at the cop and followed him out.

THIRTY-FIVE

We were sitting in the small plane waiting for take-off when it hit me.

"Why am I coming back to Spain? The job is over, you could have put me on a flight back to Edinburgh."

Fermin Benoluchi looked at me. He was back in black, his scarlet stole packed in his luggage. He looked more like himself with the trappings removed. "I never thought of it," he replied. "I have you booked out of Santander the day after tomorrow. Things have been moving so fast…"

He trailed off. I sighed. But in truth, I was not too disappointed. A day in the sun, a few hours on the beach with a good book — I could live with that. And I'd see Magda one last time. There was a spark between us. Now that the threat was lifted…? Probably not, but it was nice to fantasise.

The flight took off, and we trundled and tumbled our way back towards Spain. I am not a profiler, and neither was Fermin — funny how I thought of him as Fermin when he was out of the scarlet, and Benoluchi when he was in it. But we both knew. We had nailed the Camino Killer.

When we landed, the day was dwindling into twilight. We went to a local hotel and had a nice dinner, sharing a bottle of wine. Magda and her crew were not there.

"She's gone on. She will be in Burgos tomorrow," said Fermin. "Come along with me in the morning, and I'll get a car to bring you back to the airport on Wednesday."

So much for my day at the beach. But Burgos is one of the great cities of Spain, the sprawling medieval capital of the ancient Kingdom of Castile. The cathedral was said to be magnificent, containing important Renaissance paintings, and the city was also famous for wine, food, and the museum of evolution. *I might skip that one*, I thought. Enough to know that my ancestors were apes and my brother still was.

We ordered two shots of McCallan. A solid malt, if not the very cream. I raised my tumbler. The Spanish have no idea how to serve whisky. They just kept pouring, not that we were complaining.

"To a final day in Burgos!"

Fermin raised his and we clicked crystal. "And a night, perhaps," he grinned slyly.

Somehow I didn't think I'd be that lucky.

The following morning a small car was waiting outside the hotel, and as we were eating our breakfast the manager dropped the keys in front of the cardinal.

"Your Eminence, the tank is full," he said.

The power of the cloth.

We drove for about an hour and a half, along roads and through traffic that would have pushed my blood pressure to bursting point. Luckily, I was in the passenger seat. Fermin was used to Roman traffic, and he was enjoying the experience. Just a weekend drive for him. A game of funfair dodgems to me!

From the outside, Burgos looked like any modern industrial city in any country in Europe. The long approach road was lined each side with warehouses, factories, garages, and vague anonymous industrial buildings. Weary pilgrims trudged along, weighed down by their backpacks. We were a few hours ahead of the main rush, but some pilgrims are on the road by six a.m. and have finished that day's walk by late morning. They are the earnest walkers, who want the best bunks in the cheapest hostels.

"When you see them on a country road or a forest trail, they look so fresh. Put them on a five-kilometre concrete pavement through an industrial wasteland, and they look beat," joked Fermin.

I was disappointed by Burgos until I caught my first glimpse of the spire in the far distance. As we approached the city centre the buildings became older, with stone replacing concrete. Fermin found an underground carpark, and we abandoned the church's wheels. On foot once more, we quickly found the scallop symbols that marked the Camino. Here they were not daubed in yellow. They were discreetly woven into the fabric of the city. Every ten metres along the footpath there were brass shells embedded in the pavement. At first they were difficult to spot, but once you got the hang of it they were impossible to miss. Some were tarnished from the dirt of the road. Others were burnished by the strikes of pilgrim boots, and gleamed in the morning sun. Fermin thumbed his phone as we walked, then held it to his ear.

"Mack?"

When he hung up, he told me that the camera crew were in the square just below the cathedral, at a churros cafe. Churros are a speciality of the region — sticks of deep-fried batter dipped in luscious liquid chocolate. The breakfast of cholesterol junkies. Fermin's eyes lit up as he told me about them.

It took us fifteen minutes. We walked through the historic quarter, up a long street that sloped past luxury hotels, tourist shops and cheap cafes. The street straightened and broadened, passing the main municipal albergue, then we were looking down on the baroque extravaganza of the cathedral. We walked down the broad steps to the grounds of the huge edifice.

"It's got an original Sebastiano del Piombo," said Fermin. "Pope Clement VII hired him and his friend Michelangelo as his artists in residence. Del Piombo got the jobs outside of Rome, like the painting here."

I nodded. Interesting, but not as interesting as quaffing moist chocolate with Magda. "I'll check it out later," I said.

We walked around the side of the cathedral into the main square. A row of shops and cafes ran from one side of the cathedral towards a wide bridge that crossed the river and led to a more residential quarter of the city. Plenty of tourists, including pilgrims, mingled on the broad public space. All the cafes had chairs outside. It didn't take long to identify the chocolate shop. They had more signage than an American real estate agent. I waved across. Amanda waved back at me.

We sat at the small table and smiled across at Amanda and Mack. I looked at the empty seat.

Mack grinned. "I think Magda overdid the vino last night. She texted that she won't be with us until lunchtime."

I could feel the chance I never really had was slipping away. C'est la vie. I still had the fee.

We chatted for a while. They were planning on shooting in the cathedral for the afternoon, then driving to Sahagun, the halfway town, where they would do another few miles of walking.

"All flat," said Amanda. "Magda will like that."

I had a few of the churros, which were good but a bit rich for my taste. The coffee was ordinary. Eventually, Fermin stood. He was off to see the cathedral. I followed him. But twenty minutes of ecclesiastical treasures was enough for me. I left and walked back towards the old town. Almost immediately I found a small cafe with a pungent aroma of freshly brewed coffee. The good stuff this time. I popped them a euro and sat in the sun with an industrial strength espresso. This was living.

I was across the road from the entrance to the municipal albergue. A line of two dozen pilgrims had formed outside. Clearly the place was not open yet. So much for getting up at six and getting a start on the day. I watched in amusement as the line grew.

Then I jumped as a voice hailed me from behind, and a hand touched my shoulder.

THIRTY-SIX

Goddamn my finely honed reflexes! I spun, my hand instinctively going for my hip, where there was no gun.

"Paul," the voice had said.

Who the hell was Paul? Oh yes, my operational name. And who the hell knew my operational name? So far, everyone had ignored my attempts to conceal my identity behind a nom de guerre.

As my first hand went for a gun that wasn't there, my second hand had risen to face level, my palm facing the potential attack, my fingers bent like a claw. A quick strike and I could have both eyes out. Or at the very least painfully rack my attacker's cheek. That's what hours of running attack and defence drills in the dojo does to you.

But I have a brain that works very fast in an emergency situation. Hardly had I raised my claw than I straightened my fingers and transformed them into a pleasant wave.

"How are you doing…?" I grinned, the words coming out a bit like the annoying Joey from the annoying *Friends* sitcom. In my defence, my brain was frantically flicking through a Filofax of faces, trying to put a name to the slim young woman smiling pleasantly at me.

Then I had it.

"…Liz."

It was the woman I had met on my first night, the woman who had secured my pilgrim passport, then directed me down the wrong path the following morning, leading to my mugging.

Liz flopped down on the empty seat beside me. That is one of the drawbacks of the Camino. People tend to assume you are as friendly as they are.

"I'm a bit surprised to see you here. I thought you'd give up after a few days."

I raised an eyebrow.

"It's just, you were so under-prepared," she said. "You had no gear, and a bloody suitcase."

"I've swapped that now for a rucksack, and I bought some boots," I replied.

"No blisters?"

I sometimes forget that normal people blister when they break in new boots. Guys in my line of work rarely blister. We buy the right boots on day one, and we double sock. I wear very thin ladies' ankle socks, made from the same material as tights, under my regular wool mix hiking socks, and I never blister. Try escaping from a hit, with a team of cops or worse on your tail, with a badly blistered heel and you will know why I get these things right.

"Vaseline," I said. "Or KY Jelly if I'm stuck. WD40 in extremis."

She smiled vaguely, not sure if I was making some sort of obscure joke. "Are you staying in the hostel?" she said, nodding towards the growing crowd outside the municipal albergue.

"It looks a bit crowded to me," I replied.

"And they have the reputation of being the rudest hostel on the pilgrimage. But the beds are eight euros a night, so I will be booking in once they open. But I don't fancy standing in line after walking all morning."

I raised a hand and the waiter reluctantly came out of the cafe. We ordered a beer and a glass of red wine, and chatted about our experiences along the trail. Or at least, she did. I listened, nodding along. I threw in the odd anecdote myself, but mine weren't real experiences. I couldn't very well top her story of meeting two white cats at an abandoned barn by telling her I had watched a serial killer jump off a cliff after exchanging shots with me.

"You've forgiven me for the practical joke on the first day?" she asked tentatively.

Interesting. When I had bumped into her in Pamplona, she had insisted I had misheard her instructions. Now it was a practical joke. It confirmed my suspicion that I had been targeted, rather than being the victim of a random mugging.

I smiled. "Water under the bridge. Whose idea was it anyway?" I kept my voice casual, all traces of interest carefully concealed. But inside my heart was beating, and I could feel a slight adrenaline surge. I reminded myself that the killer was dead and this was just tying up loose ends. But the fight or flight response does not listen to reason. I surreptitiously slowed my breathing to bring my responses under control.

"A friend of yours approached me after breakfast. He said you were always playing pranks on each other and he wanted to get you lost in the forest, after you had filled his car with diesel on a road trip you did last summer."

I smiled. "I wondered when he'd get payback!" I said cheerfully, all the time wondering what the hell was going on. "It sounds like Charlie alright. Tall guy with glasses?"

Obviously Georg Fleischmann had found out that I had been hired as Magda's security detail, and had decided on a pre-emptive strike. I would have to have a word with the cardinal and with Rodriguez about security. I use fake names for a reason.

A look of uncertainty crossed her face. "No, I wouldn't have said tall," she said. "More short than anything, but not a dwarf. More Tom Cruise short than Snow White short, if you know what I mean."

I didn't bother pointing out that it was the seven dwarves who were short, not Snow White. Partly because it didn't matter, and partly because I was now looking as confused as she was. "Charlie is tall," I corrected her. Then it hit me; he might have got one of the muggers to approach her. Basic tradecraft; don't expose yourself unless you have to. It was an easy matter to sort out.

I took out my phone and quickly pulled up a picture I had taken the first time I had seen Georg Fleischmann, on the evening out with Magda in Pamplona. I had snapped the picture covertly, but the image was good. I passed across the phone.

"That's not him," she said. "It looks nothing like him."

It must be one of the two muggers, I thought.

But then she added: "Your other friend. The one you were walking with when I met you in Pamplona."

Now I was thoroughly confused. I cast my mind back. I was loitering at the edge of Magda's first press event at the cemetery when I had spotted Liz going into the hostel. I was still there a few minutes later when she came out again, and I had confronted her about her bad directions. Who was walking with me?

"The dapper guy," she added. "The one who looks like a tailor's dummy."

I felt a cold chill run down my spine. Running the images through my head, there was only one man who could be described as dapper. And that was Victor Rodriguez. Surely not? Of course not.

I took back my phone and called up a shot — a happy tourist shot of Rodriguez and Fermin with Magda enjoying a roadside coffee.

"Yes, that's him," she said excitedly, jabbing the image of the cop. Then she looked at the image more carefully. "Is that the porn star I keep hearing about? I heard she is doing the Camino topless."

"Don't believe everything you hear. She looks fully dressed to me," I said. I stood. "It was great to meet you again, but I have to meet a man in the cathedral at noon, and I am already late. Until next time, buen Camino."

I found Fermin in the oldest part of the cathedral, a small side chapel dating from the eleventh century. The stone walls were rough and the floor uneven. He was seated at a wooden pew, his eyes closed. I sat beside him.

"You move quietly," he said, without opening his eyes. "Like a cat." He sighed gently. "This is the oldest part of the church. I love to sit here and imagine the past. Men left here for the Crusades a thousand years ago. When they rose to follow El Cid and drive the Moors out of Europe, they called in here for absolution first. Sailors from the Armada that failed so dismally against your country gathered to pray here, too. It humbles me to sit here in their presence."

I am not one for ghosts, so I let that slide. I could imagine the past but I could not feel it.

After a few minutes, he opened his eyes and smiled. "You did not come here for history."

"No. I got some worrying information that throws disturbing light on the security of our investigation."

He sighed and stood. "We will go outside and discuss it. This is sanctified ground."

We went back to the churros cafe. I contented myself with bottled water. We found a quiet corner inside, and we sat.

"You remember I was mugged on the first day, the walk into Roncesvalles?"

He nodded.

"I was set up. I bumped into the woman who had directed me down the wrong path, and she admitted she had been asked to do that."

"Fleischmann?" asked the cardinal in surprise.

"No. Inspector Victor Rodriguez. He's the one who set up that attack on me."

He went pale. "That makes no sense."

"I agree. He may not have been happy to have me along for the ride, but there were other ways of dealing with that. He could have just put his foot down and refused permission."

"He seemed enthusiastic," said Fermin.

That squared with my first impression.

"We need to talk to him," I said. "We need to get to the bottom of this. If it's professional jealousy or something equally inane, I will just let it go. But until we have a discussion, it's a loose end."

Fermin took out his phone and punched in Rodriguez's number. After several quiet trills it rang out. "Odd," he said quietly. "He usually picks up immediately."

"Perhaps the morphine…?"

"No. They were weaning him off that. And he said he was going back to work. I don't think he is sleeping off the pain. I'll try his office."

He dialled a new number, and after a few rings the call was picked up. He spoke in rapid Spanish, and beyond *Hola* at the start, I didn't catch any of it. He ended with a *Ciao* — not Spanish — and hung up.

"He's not in. He rang yesterday and took a week's holiday leave."

"To recover?"

"They didn't know about his broken leg."

We looked at each other blankly, then I asked him to ring Magda. The call went through to her voicemail. Then he rang Mack.

"Hi mate, how's your didgeridoo doing?" came the cheery voice.

"Just checking, Mack — is Magda with you?"

"No. You remember she was taking the morning off. She'll meet us at two."

"She's not answering her phone."

"It's nearly one. She's probably in the shower. She'll get back to you."

I shook my head, and Fermin caught my worry.

"We're going to the hotel," he said, and hung up the phone.

THIRTY-SEVEN

It was a five-minute walk, and we made it in three. The hotel was a beautiful stone building on a corner and when we stepped in, it was like stepping back into the 1930s. An air of genteel elegance pervaded the lobby. An American couple was at the small reception desk, and the one receptionist was dealing with them. I stood impatiently, but Fermin walked right up to the desk and reached under the collar of his T-shirt, pulling out his crucifix. The receptionist caught the gesture and turned a professional smile on him.

"One moment, Father."

He smiled. "Just checking the room number of one of my party. Maria Vogt…?"

It was the name Magda was travelling under.

The receptionist looked unhappy to be disturbed while dealing with the Americans, but she quickly scanned the reservation book and said: "Room 307, third floor."

We hit the button for the elevator but it did not arrive immediately, so we took the stairs. Two at a time. We reached the third floor and quickly found the right door. I knocked, hard.

No answer.

I was knocking for the second time when Mack, slightly out of breath, appeared on the corridor. Behind him was Amanda.

"Mate, what's your worry?" he asked. But his face clearly betrayed that he felt some panic too.

"Can't be too careful," I replied. "Probably nothing, but we just want to check."

Magda had not answered my second knock.

"I'll go down to reception and get the key," said Fermin.

"Not sure they'd give it to you, not without cause anyway," I said. "Quicker I just open it myself."

I took a pen out of my pocket and unscrewed the middle. In the space normally occupied by the refill there were half a dozen thin picks. I took out the most likely and inserted it in the lock. I jiggled it a little then removed it, and tried the next. The third felt right. Then I removed the clip from the top of the pen and inserted the end in the top of the lock. I applied gentle tension as I jiggled the pick a little. It took about six jiggles to engage all four tumblers inside the lock, then I applied more pressure on the clip, and the lock slowly turned. There was a satisfying click, and the door opened inwards in response to my push. Mack gave a small cry of delight.

"Fair play, man. I didn't think it could be done that easily."

I wasn't listening. I stepped into the room and looked around.

Magda was a neat freak, which surprised me. Everything was in its place. The copy of *Marie Claire* magazine on the coffee table was aligned with the edge of the table. The used towel was folded neatly over a radiator to dry. Beyond that, there was no indication that she had ever stepped through the door. She would have been an easy house guest.

It took only a moment to establish she was nowhere in the room, or in the adjoining bathroom. Her luggage was also missing. It was in the bathroom that we found the letter. It was in a plain white envelope and addressed to Amanda. She looked at each of us in turn, then handed it to me.

I took it by the edge. Something told me this could be a piece of evidence, and I did not want my prints on it. I went back to the bedroom and found a spoon by the coffee-making facilities. I inserted the handle in the envelope and slit it open. I didn't want to tear the flap, because there might be DNA evidence from the saliva of whoever had sealed it. That's how my mind was working. I was certain this letter would contain bad news.

I let the letter slip from the envelope and used the spoon to open it out. Another surface I didn't want my prints on. The irony was that my prints were all over the room, so it was a moot point.

Once the letter was open, I could feel the others congregating at my back. I didn't try to keep the contents from them. Whatever we were about to see we were all part of. The message was brief.

Hi Amanda.

Hi all — I know you'll show this to them, Amanda.

I am very sorry. My mother has been rushed to hospital with gallstones, and I need to be with her. And if I am honest, the events of last night have upset me. I don't know if I am right for this project anymore. I'll be in touch in a few weeks. Sorry for wasting all your time.

Love, Magda XXX

"That's that," said Fermin, relief flooding through his voice. "She's gone home. I don't get a goodbye hug, but at my age a goodbye hug might have pushed my blood pressure too much. She's a nice woman. I hope she comes back to complete the pilgrimage. It would have changed her."

I didn't know what to feel. It made sense, on one level. People do get very upset after violent incidents. Post-traumatic stress is very real, and most of us lack the resources to deal with it. In combat situations I have seen it screw with even the strongest of men. I didn't believe the bit about her mother being hospitalised, but the rest had a ring of authenticity.

"If we can just get her on the phone to confirm that she has gone home, I can relax," I said.

"She hasn't gone home," said Amanda. "She's in big trouble."

THIRTY-EIGHT

Her reasoning was sound. Amanda was the liaison between Magda and the production company, and she had been dealing with her for months leading up to the shoot.

"We've become friends," she said. "And I know Magda well enough to know I smell a rat. She would not sign a letter *XXX*. To you, that might mean kisses. To her, it is something else. And Magda has never folded a towel in her life. She would never lay a magazine down carefully when tossing it aside works as well. We'd joke about it, and she'd say that's what maid service is for."

"House Cleaning could have been in and tidied up," Mack pointed out.

"No," I said. "They'd have removed the towel and replaced it with a clean one. They would never drape it over a radiator to dry. If Amanda is right, Magda has been taken."

The room went silent.

Thirty minutes later, we were sitting in an interview room at the main police headquarters in Burgos. A burly man with a five o'clock shadow on his face, despite it still being lunchtime, was questioning us. He didn't seem happy. I could see a crumb on his chin, and a red stain on his tie. We had clearly disturbed his meal.

"So let me get this clear," he said, his voice dripping with sarcasm. "Your friend has been missing for an hour, and she told you she's gone home to be with her mother. And you want to call in CSI?"

We had gone through our concerns twice, but he still wasn't getting why we were worried. I wanted to walk out and begin a thorough search. Sometimes action grounds you. But I knew the best place to begin the search was with the cops. And I had a suspicion that the search would bring us to Rodriguez. Why had he set me up to be mugged? Was he working with Fleischmann? And why would a cop be working with the Camino Killer?

I started again. I seemed to have become the spokesperson for the group. "We really are concerned," I repeated.

"And I really couldn't care less. If she doesn't report in with her mother tomorrow, wait 24 hours and we'll file a missing person's report. Now go. I have an important case to look into. My lunch."

This was going around in circles. Instinct told me to stand up and punch the jerk, but training dictated a calmer approach. Fortunately, Fermin had less training than me.

"You pompous piece of shit!" he suddenly roared. "Does this collar mean nothing to you? Your superintendent is a devout member of Opus Dei, and if you don't shift your fat arse and help us here, I will see to it that you serve out the rest of your miserable career issuing parking tickets in the mountains of Galicia."

Even I was stunned by the outburst. The cop suddenly straightened and a hard look crossed his face. Then it relaxed into an oily smile.

"Of course, Your Eminence. I will begin an investigation, though my experience tells me you are worrying needlessly."

He was backing down but trying to save face.

Ten minutes later, we were in the office of a police detective, who was taking our story a lot more seriously. He had examined and bagged the note Magda had left. He had got the bones of the story and was now probing more closely.

He had looked keenly at me at the start of the interview, but the cardinal had explained: "Security consultant hired by the Vatican. Don't ask." And he had accepted that.

"Is this Magda's writing?" he asked. Three of us just shrugged.

Amanda nodded. "It is, but a bit shakier than usual. And she never signed Xs after her name. I've got a number of notes from her."

"An X is just a signifier for a kiss. I wouldn't read anything into that," said Detective Alvarez.

"For her, three Xs don't mean three kisses. It's the business she's in, and she would not have signed off like that. Never."

He nodded. "So why did she do it this time?"

"I don't know. Maybe to let us know that she hadn't written the note."

"But she did write the note."

"Maybe under duress."

We parked the issue for a moment and he asked about Rodriguez. This was the subject we had been cautious about. I had not told Mack and Amanda that Rodriguez had set me up. And I had not mentioned it yet to the detective. It seemed so bizarre, and we were struggling as it was to get anyone to believe Magda had disappeared.

"We have tried to speak to Rodriguez, but he is not answering his phone, and his office says that he has taken a few days off."

Alvarez suddenly seemed to reach a decision. He straightened up and reached for a phone. "Here's how we will handle it," he said. "I will call the airports and see if there is a record of Magda travelling from here. If not, I'll have someone check the railway. Rail tickets don't need identification, but someone might recognise her if we bring a photo. We won't bother with buses at this stage. If she went back to Poland, she would not use a bus. And while that is in progress, I'll see if I can track down Inspector Rodriguez."

A slow twenty minutes dragged by. Alvarez left us and coffees were brought. And butter cookies which I was too tense to enjoy. Then Alvarez came back in, all business.

"She didn't fly out, not yet anyway. No tickets issued in her name. And a uniform on patrol at the train station has gone to all the tellers with a photo. She did not take the train. So hang the twenty-four hour wait; I think we can declare her missing."

That was something at least.

"More worrying, no one has heard anything from Inspector Rodriguez since he emailed asking for a week of leave. You say he has a broken leg?"

"Badly broken," I replied. "From a long fall."

He shook his head softly, looking a little lost. "I checked with the medical team who evacuated you from Alto del Perdón. They say he never went to hospital for treatment. They only carried out a cursory examination of him at the evacuation site, and there was no external sign of a break. No broken skin or swelling. Is it possible that he faked the injury?"

THIRTY-NINE

We got our answer two hours later. On Alvarez's instructions we went out for lunch, then came back to the station at three. He was waiting for us.

"Inspector Rodriguez is based in Leon, the capital of the region. And that is where the second killing in the series occurred. He was the first to suggest a link, and he was put in charge of the investigation. Which is why he was with you, I gather."

This was news to me. I had assumed that Rodriguez was just our liaison with the cops, not the chief investigator. He had kept that quiet. Was that why he resented my involvement? Setting me up for the mugging now made some sort of warped sense.

"Are you saying that now the case is cleared, he is just taking time off?" I asked.

"No," said Alvarez firmly. "Something is off. Officers from Leon have knocked on the door of his home, and received no answer. The curtains are closed, and neighbours say they have not seen his family in more than a week. His two children have not been in school. It is not just Rodriguez who is missing. We have applied for a warrant to break into his house. An entry team is on standby."

I was impressed.

We were led into a small operations room. There were two other men there, aside from Alvarez. One was another detective, while the other was in uniform, but a very formal and ornate uniform. The top brass were now involved. The room had a row of computer monitors. Three were switched on.

"Once the warrant is issued, the order will be given and these monitors will go live. We may find him inside a darkened room in a morphine haze from the pain of a broken leg. We may find his suitcases packed and a brochure for Disneyland Florida on the kitchen table. Or it may be more sinister. I am sorry, you won't be able to remain in the room for the raid."

Cardinal Benoluchi looked at him with a fixed gaze. Finally the man in the uniform nodded slightly, and Alvarez picked up the signal.

"Okay, the cardinal and the security expert can remain. But the rest of you will have to leave."

Mack seemed disappointed. He was seeing his travelogue morphing into something far bigger, and he didn't want to be excluded at this point. Footage was king and he didn't want to miss anything. But he reluctantly followed Amanda from the room.

As he was leaving, Alvarez called to him: "And don't forget your bag."

Mack grinned. "It was worth a shot," he said as he picked up the camera bag, which we all suspected housed a hidden camera.

Once they had left the room, Alvarez looked at both me and Fermin, before fixing his gaze on me. "Once this kicks off, you are observers. Keep your mouths shut and don't disturb us."

It was after four when the call came through. One of the three powered up monitors changed into an image of a policeman in black. He was wearing a stab vest, and looked like a SWAT veteran.

"Sergeant Lopez here. I gather I am speaking to the observation team in Burgos. Stand by for live feed."

The other two screens came to life, one showing the front of a small detached house, the second showing the rear of the same building. Both images were jumping around a lot. They obviously came from body cams, but the resolution was surprisingly good.

"The paperwork has just been delivered, and we are good to go. We will breach the front and back doors simultaneously in T-minus two minutes. Talk to you on the other side."

"Understood," said the man in the uniform, who was clearly the senior officer, even if it was Alvarez's case.

We waited out the two minutes. I counted the seconds in my head, and as I reached 119 the images on the screens went blurry as the men wearing the body cams began to run towards their targets. I focused on the front door image rather than flit from one to the other. The camera steadied near the door and I saw two men running into place carrying a small battering ram. They swung it twice, then let it slam into the door lock. The door smashed inwards and the screen showed the interior of a small hallway. The hallway was empty. The camera turned left, and my screen filled with chaotic images of a living room. I saw a sofa, a television, pictures of ducks on a wall, family photos, and some children's toys. But no sign of Rodriguez.

"Front room clear," came a voice.

The camera turned and we were back in the hallway, then in a small room that seemed to be a study. The frantic images were accompanied by a low soundtrack that featured bangs, lots of heavy breathing, and shouts from the raiders.

"Study clear."

The image on my screen was back in the hallway now, as I became aware that those in the room with me seemed to have gone very quiet. Then I heard someone mutter: "Oh fuck…"

I turned to the second screen, which had been showing images of the entry from the rear. The image was fixed on a kitchen, and a table. Around the table was seated a family of three. There were two children and a woman. The children were unnaturally still, and when I looked carefully I could see they were taped to their chairs. The woman was also taped. While the children wore calm looks, her face was frozen in horror. Where her eyes should have been there were two dark holes, and a streak of blood had oozed out of one of the gouged eye sockets and flowed down her cheek, looking for all the world like a bloody tear.

The image on the screen now focused in on the woman, and I could see a hand reaching forward to touch her throat, searching for a pulse. We all knew it was a vain exercise. The three ashen-faced figures were dead. Someone had wiped out Inspector Rodriguez's entire family.

FORTY

An hour had passed. The cardinal's face was streaked with tears, but he was under control again. My face was pale with suppressed fury. We all react in our own way.

Outside the police station there was a media scrum. On every television screen and on every radio station the lead story was the same. A policeman had gone postal and wiped out his entire family. He was now on the run, and people were warned not to approach him. Every cop in the region was mobilised, every airport and port under tight surveillance.

Actual news began to filter in, and Alvarez was feeding it to us as quickly as could reasonably be expected. I think it was a professional courtesy to me rather than the cardinal, because he wanted every possible man on Rodriguez's tail.

The information was sparse but unambiguous. Two days before joining Fermin and Magda at the start of the Camino — a plan his superiors had not approved, and were not aware of — the inspector had flown to Berlin. Business unknown. Neighbours spotted him on his return to his family home in Leon that night. He was seen leaving for work the following morning. None of his family were ever seen again.

An initial examination confirmed that the family had been dead a number of days. It was too early to determine cause of death, but it was assumed that the children had not suffered unduly. They had no bruises or other obvious marks. One of the cops had mentioned an odour near their mouths, which might have indicated they had inhaled carbon monoxide, or were poisoned in some way. But it was speculation.

The children's mother, on the other hand, had suffered. There were two bruises to her head, one to the side and one to the rear. And her hands bore signs of defensive wounds. It looked like he had struck her from behind, but not hard enough to render her unconscious. She had fought back, but the blow to the side of her head had either killed her, or left her unconscious and he had killed her in some other fashion.

Despite the tear of blood, it looked as if her eyes had been removed after her death. Had she still been alive, there would have been a lot more blood. There was no sign of the missing eyes, but the most plausible explanation was that the family dog had eaten them. There were signs of gore in his dog bowl. He had been found cowering in the bathroom, severely dehydrated after several days in the warm house.

"The stench is terrible. He's shat all over the floor. But at least he didn't eat the three corpses," said one of the team examining the house.

It was at this point that the cardinal had got up and walked out.

The family dog was now being minded by a neighbour. I don't know why I bother to mention that, but I suppose I don't like to leave loose ends.

There was clearly only one suspect. Inspector Rodriguez was known as a gun enthusiast. That surprised me, considering the quality of his throw-down. He kept a gun safe, and when the raid team finally got it open they discovered that all the weapons were missing. They didn't have an exact inventory, but from the slots in the safe they felt sure he had an automatic rifle, a pump-action shotgun, a target pistol, and a heavy-duty pistol such as a magnum. The ammunition was also gone.

In addition to those guns, he would have his service pistol. But at least he didn't have the throw-down. I hadn't returned it yet.

No one had any idea where Rodriguez had fled to, and there were no obvious clues in the house. That was as much as we knew.

Fermin and I adjourned to a hotel not far from police headquarters. I didn't think I was going to get anything new from Alvarez for the moment. Or anything much from Fermin. He was on his third brandy. I think he was a bit suspicious that I didn't need three brandies. Truth is, I am a whisky man. And besides, I had seen worse. Lots worse.

"You need to go easy," I said. "Because our job is not done. We need to rescue Magda, and we need to put the real Camino Killer behind bars."

He looked up, eyes slightly bleary. "Is Georg Fleischmann not the Camino Killer?"

I talked him through it, slowly. "No, he is not. He's a patsy set up by Victor Rodriguez, who is the real Camino Killer. When did you contact him about your plan to trap the killer?"

"Two weeks ago."

"That gave him plenty of time. I can only guess, but here is how I think it went down. Once you told him that Magda was the bait, the challenge would have been irresistible to him. Kill her as his yearly sacrifice, right under your nose and the nose of your security expert. It would have appealed to his ego.

"Magda told me there a restraining order against Fleischmann in Germany. He could have found that out easily, and made contact. He probably posed as a fellow stalker. He would have sold Fleischmann on the idea of kidnapping Magda and playing with her until they got tired of her. I don't know, but I suspect the gun he was firing on us with was one of

Rodriguez's. The two had a plan, which might have involved killing me and kidnapping Magda that night. Or maybe Rodriguez had a plan all of his own. Let Fleischmann create the diversion, then I would take him out. Once we saw his apartment in Berlin, we were convinced we had nailed the Camino Killer, and Rodriguez had all the time in the world to go after Magda without interference."

"That's devious," said Fermin.

"It makes some sort of sense," I replied. I was thinking about the sight of two men wrestling at the edge of a steep drop, and Rodriguez going over. How had they pulled that off? Someone had gone over.

Or perhaps not. It was dark. Fleischmann could have been wrestling with a tree trunk or a sack of old clothes, and could have flung that over the side. He just had to scream until it hit the ground, then cut off his cry. The illusion would have been perfect.

So all the time I was hunting Fleischmann, Rodriguez was sitting under cover, waiting until morning when he could creep out and pretend he had survived a big fall.

"A lot of planning went into it," I commented. "He was a few steps ahead of us the whole time. And now he has Magda."

Fermin called for his fourth brandy.

"That will have to be your last," I said. "We have a job to do. This isn't over until Magda is safe and Rodriguez is behind bars."

"What are the odds of Magda being alive?" His voice carried a note of querulous disbelief.

"Higher than you'd imagine. None of the kills were instant. They all took setting up, and at least one took days."

Fermin flinched, and I knew he was picturing the woman who had starved, her mouth sewn closed. But then his eyes hardened, and he straightened up. He pushed the fourth brandy away, untouched. "If you think we can save her, tell me what to do."

We returned to the police station, where Alvarez gave us an empty interview room. He brought in a laptop and fired it up. All the reports from the German police were now available to us. We began sifting through the files, focusing on the fifth notice board from Fleischmann's apartment.

"But Fleischmann is not the killer," said Fermin.

"No. But Rodriguez was setting him up, so the information on the boards came from the killer, and was accurate enough to throw the blame entirely on Fleischmann. We have to assume he wanted Fleischmann to take the fall for the final kill as well. We are going to work on the basis that whatever is on those boards reflects the thinking of Rodriguez. We'll get into his head and see if we can figure out what he has in mind for Magda."

The only real clue was a detailed map of the town of Leon. The map was centred on a residential suburb and the surrounding countryside rather than the centre of the historic city. And the map was unmarked. Not a single indication of where she might be held, or be killed.

"It doesn't tell us anything," said Fermin.

I wasn't so sure. I got up and found Alvarez. "Has the map been examined for forensics? Tested for invisible inks or other covert markings?"

"They're looking into it, but this isn't your first rodeo. You know it'll take days, or even weeks."

"Can the process be rushed?"

"I've already asked. We're as anxious to find her as you are. I'll let you know if we find anything. But don't hold your breath."

I went back to Fermin. "Is there anything about Leon that would resonate with what you know of the killer?"

He looked at me blankly. "It's a medieval cathedral city. There are lots of them throughout Europe. Nothing more than that."

"Then what sin is he illustrating?" I asked. "One journalist who denied Christ, one corrupt moneylender, one barrister who told lies, one defiler of human bodies — what is Magda guilty of?"

Fermin looked away, deep in thought. I decided to nudge his thinking.

"Lust," I said.

He looked at me in surprise.

I went on: "She's a major star in the porn industry. That is driven by lust, portrays lust, employs loose women to seduce men. What else can it be?"

He shook his head softly. "The porn industry is not about lust. It is all about greed," he said. "It is about the fantasy that you can get what you want, when you want it. You can have as many women as you like, and the industry is worth billions a year. That is greed, not lust."

It was an interesting perspective. I opened my mouth to argue, but Fermin went on: "Don't underestimate Rodriguez. There is a subtlety to his thinking. He would not go for the obvious. Greed is the sin."

"So where does that lead us?" I asked.

We both sat in silence for a few minutes, then Fermin said: "The moneylenders in the temple."

FORTY-ONE

I remembered the story. When Jesus had entered the temple in Jerusalem, he had turned on the moneylenders who used the space as their office, turning over their tables and driving them out. This had created a hatred of moneylenders in his followers, and crippled the banking industry through to the fifteenth century. Though I am sure Fermin had a more theological view.

"You are going to have to expand," I said. "Tell me how this relates to Magda."

He thought for a moment, then said: "A lot of the gospels are shorthand. They are parables, and you have to read around them and add context. For instance, the moneylenders in the temple weren't just lending money. Business deals were being done, and items bought and sold. If you want a loaf of bread, you go to a baker. But if you want to buy a farm or a house, you don't pick one off the shelf. You meet the seller and work out the deal some place. Many of those deals were done in the temple."

Light slowly dawned.

"You mean, Magda is the product being sold?"

"Let's tease it out," said the cardinal. "How would that work?"

I shrugged. There are a few ways of selling humans. Prostitution is the obvious one. Some is voluntary, some is forced. But generally no one dies. Then there is human slavery. Slavery today is big business in some parts of the world, a trade that generates $35 billion a year. Does a glum-looking Vietnamese girl do your nails before a night out? Odds are good that she was trafficked, and is not paid for her work. She may not be in chains, but she is a slave. There are roughly 30 million slaves worldwide. Somehow I couldn't see Magda being sold to a manicure franchise, though.

Then Fermin spoke again. "You hear of women and children being sold on the darknet. They are used as sexual playthings, then killed by their owners."

My heart went cold. I could see that happening. But there was one problem.

"Our killer likes to display his victims. If he sold Magda and someone else killed her, then he wouldn't be able to stage the scene."

"He might be selling her to be killed. A snuff movie."

"Those are mythical. They never happened," I said. But the world is a sick place, and everything happens for a first time. Surely not this? We were going around in circles, speculating needlessly.

"We need a few hours' sleep," said Fermin. "My head is addled. I'll see you at seven."

Next morning at seven, we checked in with the local cops. No news overnight. Fermin looked at me.

"Have you thought about my idea?"

I had thought about little else all night. It was time to take this to another level and call in the big guns.

I got my smartphone — which is not so much a phone as a sophisticated spying machine — and dialled the number of my good buddy Bill in the CIA. I have done a number of jobs for him in the past, and he helped me get out of a tight spot in Bosnia only a few months earlier. This time, all I was asking for was information.

It took longer than a normal call to connect. The level of encryption was very high, and the call was routed through a satellite rather than through the mobile network. But eventually I heard the *beep beep* that told me it was ringing at the other end. I angled my screen towards my face, and waited for the video stream to kick in.

It was after seven here in Spain, so one a.m. in Virginia. Bill was based in Langley, and lived in a small town within driving distance. I expected him to be groggy and annoyed at me disturbing his beauty sleep. God knows Bill is no oil painting; he needs his beauty sleep.

Bill was groggy alright, but not annoyed. If anything, he seemed delighted to get my call. He was sitting up in bed, his chest bare, as he answered. "How are you doing, Eliot? I presume this is a social call, because no one would call me in the middle of the night on business."

"You look happy," I remarked.

"You wouldn't believe how happy," he grinned. "Look at this." He moved the phone and I could see his new girlfriend sitting beside him in the bed.

She smiled at me. "Hi, Eliot — I'm Stacey."

"Hello, Stacey," I replied. I was impatient but I couldn't rush this. Bill was a friend, and he would help me. I would just play it cool, and conceal my frustration.

Playfully Bill pulled down the sheet, exposing Stacey's breasts. She slapped him on the wrist, but didn't bother pulling the sheet back up. A little less prudish than most Americans, I thought. And very cute.

Then Bill moved the phone again, to the other side of the bed. A sleepy young woman waved at me.

"This is Elaine. She works with Stacey. And we have just had a wonderful evening, if you catch my drift. Jealous?"

My phone screen now showed an image of a grinning Bill sandwiched between two beautiful women, looking as happy as a diabetic trapped in a sweet shop.

I moved my phone to include Fermin in the image. "Bill, I'm here with Cardinal Fermin Benoluchi. Cardinal as in Vatican bureaucrat, not as in ball player. Savvy?"

I could see the look of surprise on his face, then he slithered down and pulled the sheets up to his neck. The two girls scooted underneath the covers.

Bill blessed himself, a thing I never thought I would see him do. He is an old sinner like myself, only worse. Far worse. I grinned as I saw his discomfort.

"Give me a minute," he muttered, and the phone went down, screen to the wood, on his bedside locker. About three minutes later, the screen came alive again, and there was a bit of movement before the image settled on Bill in a shirt and tie, sitting at his chair in the study I knew so well.

"You're not wearing any trousers, are you?" I asked.

"You'll never know," he replied. "You need to give a man warning if you are going to disturb his night like that. What do you want, anyway?"

"As I was starting to tell you, I am with Cardinal Benoluchi."

I adjusted the phone until both myself and Fermin were in the image Bill could see. Fermin had a big grin on his face. Even though he did not know Bill, he clearly had enjoyed his discomfort. Bill grimaced. But he recovered his old cockiness quickly.

"Good evening, your Eminence. Or should I say good morning — you're based in Rome, aren't you?"

"You know your cardinals," said Fermin. "But at the moment, I am on temporary assignment in Spain."

Bill nodded. "I know my cardinals alright. You're Paul Marcinkus's boy."

Fermin looked pained. "Archbishop Marcinkus is dead. And when he was alive, I was not his boy. I worked briefly in his department when I was a young curate, but I was several pay grades below the level where the improprieties, if there were any, took place."

"There were plenty," said Bill. "But yeah, they weren't on your head. That was a cheap shot. So, how can I help you?"

I took over. "We are stalking a serial killer who has been targeting victims on the Camino Way," I began.

Bill leaned away from the phone for a minute, and his face was lit by the eerie light from a computer screen. He popped back up. "We don't have much on that. Four killings, no evidence they are linked beyond the coincidence of the dates of the kills. But if it is one guy, he's a nasty creep from the look of things. Our provisional profile says…" He laughed. "You won't believe this. 18% chance he is in law enforcement!"

"We know who he is. He was the lead detective on the investigation."

"No shit! I'd better update the file."

"Do it in the morning. We have more pressing concerns."

And I laid it out for him. He listened, throwing in the odd question. Finally he said: "Cardinal, you really believe greed is the way to go with this one? Not lust?"

The cardinal nodded.

"Okay. There are sites on the darknet where people are traded. Some very sick places in cyberspace. The problem is, it is the dark web. Hard to access, and if you do, the guys already there won't know you. So you will be frozen out. A darknet auction is not like an eBay auction, where anyone can follow it. But I have a guy."

"Really?" I feigned surprise, but I knew he would have a guy. He always had a guy. He was like seven degrees of separation on steroids. He was never more than a call or two away from the most depraved individuals on earth.

"What's her name again?"

"Magda Lynn."

"Never heard of her."

A female voice from behind him said: "She's a Euro-porn star, from Poland."

"Bill," I admonished, "this is a highly sensitive matter. You can't have people overhearing our conversation."

"It doesn't go beyond this room," he said. "Don't get your knickers in a twist. It will take me a few hours."

The screen went dead. Fermin and I talked for a few minutes, then he went back to bed. I stayed awake and fretted. We could do nothing more.

We were having a late second breakfast when the call finally came through.

FORTY-TWO

It was a straight voice call, and I could hear the excitement in Bill's tone. I quickly signalled to Fermin, and we retired to my room, where we would not be disturbed. I put Bill on speaker.

"We found the auction," he said, triumph in his voice.

"That's brilliant," I said.

There was a micro hesitation on the line.

"Not so brilliant?" I prompted.

"Not so brilliant. She's in a shitload of trouble."

Magda was the only lot in a very rare hunter auction, Bill explained. A hunter auction was where the bidders were hunters, and the victim was the game.

"It's an extreme form of big game hunting," Bill said. "Some rich assholes get their rocks off by paying tens of thousands to hunt and kill endangered species such as rhinos or gorillas. A few pay even more to hunt people. Miss Lynn is being put up as the bait for these hunters. The four highest bidders will have to make their way to Leon by tomorrow evening. They will be brought to a secret location, and each one will enter the kill zone from a different side. Whoever finds Magda first gets three hours to do what he likes with her, then kill her however he likes."

"And the other three?"

"They watch the kill. It is part of the thrill. But more importantly, it makes them accessories. That's important for security. You don't want a disgruntled loser complaining afterwards on Facebook."

Fermin had gone white. There was despair in his eyes, but also pure anger. He thought he knew evil, but he was only a rookie. This was depravity on a level alien to him.

"When is the auction?" I asked.

"Four p.m. today, your time."

"Could I hit the location and rescue her before that?" I didn't have much hope, but I had to ask.

"Not a chance. Not only don't we have intelligence on how many goons are guarding her, we don't know where she is being held. My guys have done a trace on the computer hosting the auction. It took a lot of effort, but in the end Rodriguez is not a tech nerd and my guys are. They broke his security wall, and traced his location to a suburb of Leon. Actually, a small village about three miles from the city."

"I could hit there."

"Grow up," said Bill. "You know he's not holding her there. And you won't get a confession and a location out of a guy like him, no matter how many toenails you put a pliers to."

"So what do I do?"

Bill sighed. "You let me do my thing. I'll have a bidder in the auction, and we'll know who the four winners are. We will track their communications until we know where the hunt is. Then you go in an hour ahead of time and rescue her."

Risky.

"And there's another thing. I can't get back-up to you. I have nobody in Europe who can reach you in time. Unless you have a colleague in the area you trust — and I wouldn't trust your colleagues — you are on your own. Could you use the cardinal?"

Fermin looked surprised at that suggestion, but said: "I will do what I can."

"No," I interrupted. "Fermin is a good man in a crisis, but this calls for special skills. If he comes along, I'll end up babysitting him and that will compromise the rescue. I'll have to do this on my own."

"No better man. I'll ring you when the auction begins."

And the line went dead.

A few hours later, we were back in my room with the phone line open.

"The auction begins in about three minutes, and my guy is ready," said Bill.

"Is he agency?" I asked.

"God, no. He's a paedophile out of Bangkok. I caught him about eight years ago, and I didn't kill him. I use him now when I want to infiltrate some highly specialist groups. Like today. He'll start the bid, then drop out. But that gives us a digital window into the auction, and I'll be able to get your location for you."

It made sense, on one level. But a better idea was beginning to form in my head.

"I need to put you on mute for a minute. The cardinal and I need to discuss something."

"Don't linger," he replied. "The auction begins in under two minutes now, and won't run more than ten. Maybe a lot shorter than that."

I didn't waste time on a reply. I muted the phone, and turned to the cardinal. "I can try to rescue her before the hunt begins, but tactically it would be easier to rescue her when the guards are distracted. If I rescue her during the actual hunt, my odds improve."

"But there will be four more guns on you."

This was the kernel of the plan.

"Three, if Bill's guy can win one of the four spots and I take his place."

It took the cardinal a moment, then he got what I proposed. "Mother of God," he said, and he crossed himself. "Are you asking the Church to bid on a human life?"

I nodded.

He shook his head. "It's like asking an undercover cop to commit a major crime. He can't."

"Sometimes he has to. Greater good."

"Morality isn't relative."

"Your call," I said. "But if you do it my way, we increase the chances of rescuing Magda hugely. And I can take three depraved human hunters out at the same time."

"No killing," he said.

"I'm not making that promise. I can try, but I can't have my hands tied. Bottom line is, Magda comes out alive. I'll make the exfiltration as clean as I can, but if there are casualties, we both know they won't be innocent people. Your conscience will have to make room for that."

He nodded, and touched my shoulder gently. "Make the call," he said.

I de-muted the phone line, and told Bill to instruct his man to stay in until the end, no matter how high it went.

Twelve seconds later, the auction began.

And eight minutes after that, a Bangkok paedophile won the third spot in the human hunt, with a bid of $128,000 of Vatican money.

I was now in The Hunger Games.

FORTY-THREE

Two hours later, we got the full report from Bill. The auction had been won by Yanis Dorf, a dentist from Chicago who had briefly been notorious on the internet for killing a lioness in front of her two cubs with a crossbow, inside a wildlife park. The second-place bidder was Johannes Strubel, South African former cop with form for violence against Blacks. He now ran his own private security company.

The third hunter was our man, Reginald Allen. He was an expat Englishman living in Bangkok, who ran go-go bars and massage parlours. He was unlikely to look much like me, so I would rely on a little help from some friends and plenty of moxie to pass for him the following day.

Our final competitor was a Canadian woman who had made her money in the tech industry. She, not surprisingly, had been the toughest one to track down. But once Bill had a name, he had plenty on her. Angie Koll was notorious for posting her kills on Facebook. She was playful about it. At Christmas she would slaughter reindeer. At Easter, cute bunnies who bled a lot. You get the picture.

Those were the people I was competing against. Not the nicest bunch of chums I had ever hung out with, but surprisingly not the worst. I had about a day to get ready for the contest. There would be no more help from Bill. He could potentially still find the location of the hunt, but as I was being brought there anyway, that was now moot. A map of the location would have been nice, but as no one else had that either I was under no disadvantage. It was now a battle of wits, and I knew — I hoped — that I was the best killer out there.

We were given minimal information from the hunt organisers. We had to make our own way to Leon, and we would be picked up once we arrived. We would be issued with our weapons and dropped at the hunt site. Then we had three hours to find Magda, and the winner would have two hours with her. After that we'd make our own way home.

"One thing bothers me," I said to Fermin. "He has always staged the killing up to this. A hunt is too random. Someone else carries out the killing, and he has no control over the method."

Fermin thought for a moment, then said: "He has control over location, though. Perhaps that's the key?"

Could be. I worked it out in my head. He might not control the method of killing, but he could control what was found afterwards. He could stage the corpse. All his killings had been symbolic, and the death scenes were tableaux that illustrated the message. If his message was greed and the expulsion of the moneylenders from the temple, how would he depict that in Magda's death?

I asked Fermin.

"The temple crops up a number of times in scripture, not just in that story," he replied. "The temple was destroyed in Solomon's time, and was restored. Many theologians take Christ as the living embodiment of the restoration of the temple."

Something pinged in my head. "He's going to bring down the temple. That's his plan. This will be his most spectacular killing yet. He is going to literally drop a building on Magda and the four people hunting her."

"How in blazes will he do that?" asked Fermin incredulously.

There was the rub. He couldn't actually drop a building on us. Or could he?

"We need to check if there are any big industrial buildings scheduled for demolition in the next few days," I said.

It took an hour. Bill worked on it, and I worked on it. Bill strode the information superhighway, looking at public records and planning applications. I tracked down a local journalist in Leon and said I was a videographer and I had heard there was a controlled explosion scheduled for the next few days. He told me when and where.

Almost immediately my phone rang. It was Bill. "I've found your location," he began.

"Yes, an old generating station in the hills above Leon. It's due for demolition by controlled explosion at nine in the morning the day after tomorrow, about three hours after our hunt ends. We'll be found weeks or months later, when they sift through the rubble."

"I don't know why I bother helping you," he laughed, and slammed down the phone.

FORTY-FOUR

We moved to Leon that evening. Along with Burgos and Pamplona, it is one of the major cities on the Camino. We had parked in a huge underground facility. The centre of the town is car free. An elevator brought us up from the parking bay into a magnificent sixteenth-century piazza, and the hotel was off that, a few minutes' walk from the cathedral and the tourist centre of the city.

I woke on the morning of the hunt with a tight knot in my stomach, and had to force myself to eat a light breakfast. It was important that my system buzzed with energy. Bill had illegally diverted a high-altitude drone from Syria, and he did a few flybys over the power plant. The drone was fitted with a heat-seeking camera, and it detected no hot spots.

"She's not there yet," he reported. So no chance of a pre-emptive strike to free her before the games began. I would have to wait it out and go in with the others. Fermin insisted I walk with him up to the gothic cathedral that dominated the town. I couldn't find an excuse not to. He was dressed in black, and carried a small briefcase.

"Indulge me," he said.

We got to the church, and as we were about to enter, my phone binged. I looked down in disgust. Another message from my brother.

Fermin smiled. "Whatever sins he is contemplating, they are small beside what you and I have committed and are committing," he said. "Cut him some slack and don't be judgemental. When this is over, give him a call and get the full story."

I was surprised. "I didn't tell you about…"

"Magda did. I'm like her gay friend." He indicated the collar around his neck. "She confides in me. She finds you cute, by the way. Now come inside. We have one thing to do to prepare you for tonight."

We entered the huge wooden door and were dwarfed by the high ceiling and the huge pillars. We walked up the left aisle, and found a small side chapel. It was locked behind an ornate brass gate. As we reached it, a small balding priest walked up to us.

"Your Eminence, it is ready," he said, turning a key and opening a small door in the brass gate.

Fermin stepped through, and gestured me to follow. "Thank you," he said. "We won't need long."

The priest seemed a little put out to be dismissed so rapidly, but he walked away.

Fermin turned to me. "I am going to say Mass. And before you object, I say a very quick Mass."

"I'm not Catholic."

"I can still pray for your soul, and mine."

He opened his briefcase and took out a small silver chalice and some other altar ornaments. He also removed a green and gold scarf, which he draped over his shoulders. Finally, he removed a worn and well-thumbed black breviary and opened it.

He was as good as his word. It took about twenty minutes, and he didn't offer me the host. I didn't even try to offer responses in the appropriate places, though I could have joined in the Lord's Prayer if I had a mind to. I know that one.

Finally it was over. I felt a bit lighter as I walked out of the church behind him.

Like Fermin, I had my own preparations to make. My preparations brought me not to a church, but to a circus.

I walked under the glowing proscenium arch at the entrance to the big top. Spelt out in glowing neon was the legend *Cirque Petrograd — The Official Soviet Circus. About as official as a three pound note*, I thought. But the talent was real. Twenty metres above me a slim, dark-haired woman was slowly pacing across a high wire. Her long legs were straight and her calves taut, emphasising every beautiful line. She combined the grace of a ballerina with the strength of a wrestler. When she reached the middle of the wire, she paused to remove three balls from a small pouch by her waist. She began with a simple up and down cascade, but then her hands blurred as she moved into a Mills Mess, one of the most graceful moves any juggler can make. It takes months of constant practice to nail the moves on the ground. How much time had she spent to be able to do it perched three storeys up?

She caught the balls gracefully, and restored them to the pouch. Then she raised her arms above her head and fell over backwards.

I felt a visceral thrill as she fell through the air, but the safety net caught her, and she bounced, landing lightly on her feet. Then she gripped the edge of the net and swung down to the ground.

It was then that she spotted me. "Eliot!" she screamed in excitement. She leapt into my arms, wrapping her strong legs around the small of my back. I felt the familiar tingling... The things we had done. If her husband only knew.

But they were both free spirits, and I suspected he knew well. It had not dented our friendship.

"Business or pleasure?" she asked.

"It's always a pleasure to see you, but this is business, I'm afraid. I need to see Stromboli."

Five minutes later, I was in the large camper van that The Great Stromboli shared with Elaina, the Queen of the Air. Stromboli — everyone called him that — was a fire-eater, sword swallower, and strong man. A Cossack, he claimed to be descended from Taras Bulba, the revolutionary leader. I took this claim with a grain of salt, as I knew Taras Bulba was a character in a Gogol novel. But Stromboli was noted for more than his talent and doubtful lineage. What made him stand out was his appearance. His body was covered with hundreds of long scars and slashes. While some people are obsessed with tattoos or body piercings, it was through scars and burns that Stromboli expressed his individuality. Each to their own, I suppose.

His face was also covered with scars. But what the public did not know was that the scars on his face were not real. He was one of the world's leading experts on special effects make-up, often being paid big bucks to take a week off the circus and work on a Hollywood blockbuster.

I showed him a photograph. "I need to look like him," I said.

He looked at the picture. It showed a man with bright red hair, a wispy goatee, and a deep scar across his face, crossing over his eye. "Bottle?" he asked.

"I think he was glassed," I confirmed. "He's a nasty creep, and I am sure he deserved it."

He chewed his lower lip for a moment, then nodded. "Yes, I can do it. No problem."

An hour later, a fast car brought me from the circus to Valladolid, and deposited me at a railway station. Then it turned and pulled off at great speed for Leon, the final stop along the line. I waited thirty minutes, and the train from Madrid arrived. I found the third carriage from the front — first class, of course — and my man was in the fourth seat, just like he said he would be. I couldn't miss him. He was wearing a lime green shirt over tan chinos, and a black beanie hat over a shock of red hair. He would have stood out at a clown convention. Except for the scar. No clown would have that.

Reginald Allen, Bangkok businessman, notorious paedophile, and winner of the third spot in tonight's hunt. I could feel my skin crawl just walking by him, but I suppressed it. There was work to do. I nodded imperceptibly at him, and he stood and followed me down the carriage.

We reached the toilet at the end of the carriage. No one was looking, and we slipped in.

I took off my Grateful Dead T-shirt and handed it to him. He looked at it like it was so much dirt, but he slipped off his green number and handed it to me. He put on a dark wig I had brought for him, and took off his glasses. Then, reluctantly, he took the electric razor I handed him and shaved the goatee. He wouldn't pass for me, not in a million years. But neither did he look like the guy who had got on the train from Madrid airport. He left the toilet and found a new seat, losing himself in second class.

Meanwhile, I set to work. Greasing my hair flat, I positioned the skull cap Stromboli had given me, then doused it with medical adhesive and applied the reddish wig he had provided. Then, the goatee. Finally, the fake scar, which crossed through my eyebrow convincingly before furrowing into my cheek.

Confident of my disguise, I left the toilet, returning to Allen's vacant seat in first class. I didn't believe for a moment I could have passed for him, but no one in Spain knew him, so it was good enough.

When the train arrived at Leon, the plan was for Allen to slip quietly out and get into the fast car, which also contained Cardinal Benoluchi. He would remain hidden until all this was over. It wouldn't help my chances of saving Magda if there were two Reginald Allens seen in Leon.

I dismissed him from my thoughts, closing my eyes and focusing on my breathing, trying to find the zone that would ground me for whatever was to come. In the end, it was simple. You worry, you die. You don't worry, you die. So why worry? I relaxed. Time flew. Before I knew it, the tinny voice over the Tannoy announced Leon, and I stood. Game on.

My heart was in a flutter. Facing death is a funny thing. It hits us all differently. Some guys get into a funk and lose the plot completely. Some guys blank out. A few just don't care. I fall in the middle. The day before, I am in a bit of a tizzy. My heartbeat is elevated, and my head is full of crazy worries. It's like the anticipation normal people feel as they walk into a funfair and approach the biggest rollercoaster. But once it starts, my focus becomes like a laser. It's all about the mission. External thoughts disappear. Time seems to slow down. My reaction time sharpens. Adrenaline is my high-performance super-drug.

I was still in the worry phase when I stepped off the train. The biggest worry was that Rodriguez would be there to meet me. My disguise was good, but I was not sure how much scrutiny it would bear. I had decided that Reginald Allen would have a Cornish accent. I have a good friend from Cornwall and hoped I could do the accent. If that passed muster, the wig might not come in for too much scrutiny. Thankfully, Rodriguez was not a native English speaker, which would help.

As it turned out, I needn't have worried. Rodriguez was not at the station waiting for me. Instead, there was a short stocky man in a baseball cap. I recognised him immediately. It was one of the two men who had mugged me on the first day of my Camino. This was a surprise, but not a wholly unpleasant one. If Rodriguez was hiring these guys again, it meant he had a limited pool of talent to draw on. And I had beaten these guys before. I could do it again. It made the job of exfiltrating Magda a little easier.

We had briefly considered alerting the police and leaving the job to them. But we had rejected it, because it put her life in too much danger. Not only would Rodriguez and his thugs be at the hunt site, there would be three armed hunters. It was too dangerous having cops blunder in with limited intelligence. I would go in as one of the hunters, find her, take out the other hunters, and effect the rescue. Hopefully without killing, but I had not made that promise. I am not a politician; I don't make promises I might not be able to keep.

I walked down the platform from the train and approached my mugger. He was wearing a scarlet jacket and a baseball hat, as we had been told, so even if I had not recognised him, I would have known who to aim for.

I walked confidently. It was unlikely he would recognise me. We had only met once before, and that was in a dark wood with plenty of blows being exchanged. No time to register faces properly. And now I was a redhead, in a loud Hawaiian shirt.

The other thing that helped was that he wasn't looking at me. He was looking at another competitor who had stepped from the train behind me. I had spotted her, but ignored her. Experience has shown me it is better to let your competitors think you are an unobservant fool.

Now I turned and looked at her openly. It was Angie Koll, the woman who liked posing with her kills on Facebook. On

Facebook she was cute. In the flesh she was spectacular. She stood a little over six foot tall, with a wave of soft red hair — genuine, unlike mine — cascading down her shoulders. Her eyes were brown, and her lips full and inviting. She had curves in all the right places, and plenty of them.

"Wow!" whispered my mugger. "An Amazon."

I didn't bother pointing out that the Amazons of mythology had cut off one breast to facilitate speedy archery, whereas Angie could have nursed a small nation from either side. I concurred with his sentiment. This was a spectacular woman.

She smiled, and my knees went a little weak. If someone had mentioned Magda to me right then, I would have said: "Magda who?"

"Hi. I'm Angie," she said to me, extending a hand.

"I'm Reggie," I replied. I saw a look of disdain cross her face as she registered me as the in-house paedophile. She had obviously broken their security like I had and checked out her fellow competitors. She took back her hand and turned away from me. Had I made my first enemy before the game had even begun?

FORTY-FIVE

We were driven, in funereal silence, across the city and out into the countryside. We drove about two miles along a small road lined with olive groves, and finally arrived at a single-storey farmhouse. Another car was already there. We went around the rear of the house and entered a rustic kitchen. Rodriguez and my other mugger were seated at a table enjoying fresh bread brushed with olive oil. There were bowls of soup in front of them. I presume it was my other mugger. The last time we had met he was in biker leathers, so it was hard to be sure. Two other people were seated at the table.

Rodriguez smiled as we entered. "First names only," he said. "For security." He rose and gestured us to chairs. "Our newcomers are Angie and Reginald."

"Reggie," I said in my mock Cornwall accent. Everyone at the table ignored me. They were all looking at Angie. But I had looked into their faces as I was introduced, and no one had flinched at my name the way Angie had. Good to know — the other two competitors had not tried to check out their opposition. I took a moment to examine them as Rodriguez gave their first names. Bill had already given me the rest.

Johannes Strubel was thin and wiry, and never seemed to stop moving. Even in repose some part of his body was constantly twitching. Hyperactive. Guys like him have fast reactions and are men of action. But they are easy to creep up on. Good to know.

The final competitor was slightly plump, but in the hard way some ex-athletes are. You could tell he had put on a few pounds, but you could hit those pounds with a baseball bat and the bat would break. Yanis Dorf, the big game dentist. Not used to prey that bit back.

Rodriguez introduced himself as Victor. This reinforced my belief that we were not meant to survive the night. Had this contest been as advertised, he would have used a fake name to protect himself. He barely looked at me. It felt a little humiliating to be looked down on by a serial killer, but there are hierarchies of evil, and a paedophile occupies a very low rung. I shrugged it off. This was on Reggie, not on me. As myself they might have loved me. Not that it mattered. I was not looking for friends.

After our soup Rodriguez left, returning a few minutes later with two bags. He opened the smaller of the bags first. It contained four Beretta 87 target pistols, with full clips. Ten rounds of .22. No stopping power unless you got the aim exactly right.

"No one will have an advantage," he grinned, as he handed out the weapons. Then he opened the second, bigger bag. "Each of you can choose a second weapon. Just one."

He spilled the contents out on the table. There were two small crossbows, a compound bow, some hunting knives, a spear gun, and a taser.

Johannes grabbed the compound bow immediately. Interesting. So he knew Angie liked the bow, and he decided to deprive her of her favourite weapon. He had done his homework after all. She smiled pleasantly, then walked over to him and took the bow off him. She turned away. He let her. First battle lost.

Looking slightly foolish, he took one of the two crossbows. It came with a quiver of four bolts, just like Angie's bow had four arrows.

Yanick Dorf took a sharp hunting knife. I looked at the remaining weapons. I could have gone for the remaining crossbow, but I don't live in the fourteenth century. I could have gone for a hunting knife, but I thought it would be as easy to take Dorf's once the game began. I took the taser instead.

Rodriguez repacked the remaining weapons. "Two more things," he said. "We will need to take your phones, for obvious reasons. So no selfies with dead bodies!"

He laughed, and we all laughed politely, as we put down our phones on the table.

"That just leaves the rules. At ten p.m., just half an hour after nightfall, you will all be brought to the hunting ground. It is a large industrial building, completely empty and isolated. You will be let in through different entrances and at different times, but all within a few minutes of each other. You will have until one a.m. to find Magda Lynn. Once you find her, you ring the bell beside her, and the game is over. You have the next two hours to do as you will. When you are finished, you ring the bell a second time and we will all join you. For the kill. None of us want to miss the kill, do we?"

He looked around. Angie Koll was smiling excitedly. Dorf the dentist was sweating and looked pale. It had suddenly become very real to him. Strubel, aside from his constant twitches, seemed unmoved. I kept my poker face.

"Once you are let into the building, anything goes," Rodriguez went on. "Within reason. Remember, there will be a clean-up afterwards. Don't give me too much work. But it is a game to the death. If you choose to target your fellow competitors, that is within the rules. Just remember, if you try to kill them, they can try to kill you. Are you prepared for that?"

Angie Koll looked daggers at me. She had made her call on that issue already.

Rodriguez looked at Dorf, who had shrunken within himself. "Don't worry. The previous times we played this game no one got hurt, aside from the target. Hunting is a sport for gentlemen. And beautiful ladies."

Dorf smiled weakly, pretending to look relieved.

Struble grinned. "First time for everything," he said.

I would get Bill to check, but I was fairly sure there had been no previous hunts. We were the first — and last — for this particular gentleman's game.

After a full security pat-down, we were dismissed to our rooms to prepare. The house was deceptively large, with a row of small bedrooms in an annex at the rear. We each had a narrow single bed, a chair, and a table to lay out and prep our weapons. I left the room twice. Once to have supper around seven, and once around eight-thirty to use the bathroom. After locking the door, I sat carefully on the bowl and squeezed out a small bowel movement. When I heard the plop, I turned and examined the contents of the bowl.

If you have never been to prison, smuggled drugs, or been a hitman, you will never have done anything like this. Lucky you: it is disgusting.

I fished in the toilet bowl with a pencil, and found it quickly. A small condom, tied at the end. Inside the condom was the world's smallest commercially available phone. It is the L8star mini phone, barely the size of your thumb. I had purchased one the previous day, then wrapped it in the condom and inserted it up my rectum on the train from Madrid. Now I carefully removed it from the condom, and dropped the condom back in the bowl. I flushed away the evidence, then washed my hands. Three times.

Back in my room, I sent a text through to Bill: *Game begins at ten.*

He was going to run the drone by the site a few times during the night, but there was little else he could do. He couldn't even track my phone, because it wasn't a smartphone. But at least I knew I could call in the cavalry immediately once I had rescued Magda.

Now all I had to do was wait for the starter's gun.

FORTY-SIX

A little before ten, we were all put in the back of a darkened van. There was an air of suppressed excitement among us, as if we were all about to embark on a parachute jump together. At ten, Strubel was taken from the van. We couldn't see much, and the door was immediately closed. We drove for another five minutes, and Dorf was removed. He might have been left in the same entrance as Strubel, or a different one. We didn't know. That left just Koll and I in the back of the van. In the dark light, I could sense her eyes boring into me. The van slowed.

"I'm going to kill you," she hissed.

I feigned hurt. "I was going to invite you to dinner," I replied.

Then the van stopped and the door opened. I was removed and brought over to a small side door in a big concrete wall. The door was open. I stepped through, and the door shut behind me. I was in the game.

To move or not to move?

If I moved, was someone waiting for me? I didn't believe anyone would really try to kill me. Aside, of course, from our ginger Amazon. But that was personal. She didn't like me. And she was still in the van.

I stood with my back to the wall beside the gate and surveyed my surroundings. I was in a small yard, with a few barrels to one side. Facing me was a closed door into the main building. I looked up. I could see a few early stars, with clouds scudding across the sky. Somewhere way above me a drone could be looking down, but there was no way I could see it from down here. I could be alone, except I knew that two hunters were already inside. And the fourth would be, in a few minutes. There was no time to linger.

I checked the yard quickly, then went to the door and tried the handle. It moved. Slowly I eased it open and slipped through, sliding along the wall. I got into shadow as quickly as I could, so as not to present too easy a target.

I could see nothing, so I began moving along the wall, trying my best not to make any noise and to keep in the shadows. I had three tasks. Incapacitate the three hunters. Take out Rodriguez. Save Magda. In that order. There was no point in rescuing Magda, only to be caught in the crosshairs of a crossbow.

I forced myself to be systematic. Searching a space without a plan normally results in you covering the same ground many times while missing spots completely. We have an instinct to go in circles, and we all have blind spots. So I decided to circle exclusively to the left. Assuming the other hunters explored the areas around their entrance points first, I might come into their zones and steal a march on them.

Of course, it is never that easy. I circled to my left, and quickly reached a wall. A quick recce showed me I was in a medium-sized room, and the room was empty. So I opened the door opposite to where I had been put in, and entered a large factory floor. And I began moving left, keeping to the shadows. Stick to the plan.

I was light on my feet, careful not to make a sound. Five minutes passed. The room was huge, almost the size of a football field. The centre of the room was dominated by eight large machines. These must be the generators, which meant I was in the heart of the power station. It was a coal-powered plant, so under each generator would be a huge reservoir for burning coal. Above would be the water tank, and above that the turbines and the generators themselves. Magda could be in any part of any of the eight generators. Or she could be in the coal storage buildings. Or the administrative block. It was going to be a long night.

Five minutes into my stealthy creep through the generating room, I heard a scraping noise and I froze. It might be rats. But I didn't think so.

Dropping low, I strained to identify where the scraping was coming from. It seemed to be from one of the generators. They were in two rows of four, and I thought it was coming from the further away row. So I kept low and made my way to the first row, crouching behind one of the massive machines. The sound seemed to be coming from my right — possibly the second or third generators in the next row. I listened for a few minutes until I was sure, then I slowly made my way around the side of the generator. When I got to the end, I peered out. Jackpot. I didn't think it would be that easy. I had located the first of the hunters.

FORTY-SEVEN

Yanis Dorf, the pudgy dentist, was climbing a ladder that led to a metal platform around the top of a generator. The generator was about thirty feet high, and the platform he was making for was about twenty feet up. It should have been a great vantage point, and perhaps that was what he thought. But he would soon find the other seven generators obstructed the view. And while he climbed the ladder, his back was to me. I took a quick look around, then swiftly crossed the gap, my rubber-soled shoes making no sound.

He reached the platform and began moving around to the right. Once he was out of sight, I quickly made my way up the stairs to the platform and moved left. I walked along the length of the generator, and stood about a foot from the corner, back to the cold metal of the machine. I could hear his breathing and the shuffle of his feet.

He had rounded the far end of the generator and was about to come around the corner into my sight. I tensed. I had my taser at the ready. I might not have to use it. I would be flexible.

He came around the corner fast but relaxed, a silly grin on his face. He looked like some kid playing paintball. When he saw me, his face froze for a moment, then his grin broadened. "Great minds think alike," he said.

"And fools seldom differ," I finished.

He looked puzzled. I let it go as I slipped the taser back into my jacket pocket. I didn't think it would be needed.

He looked around, like Ahab on the topmast of the Pequod. Then he said: "That talk about us all being allowed to hunt each other, it got me a bit jittery. It was suddenly very real."

"What did you expect?" I asked.

"I don't know — some sort of cross between hide-and-seek and laser tag. I don't even know why I signed up. I thought she would be roaming through the building and we would be hunting her. I didn't think she'd be held someplace, and we'd have to kill her in front of everyone. That seems like murder on some level."

On every level, mate.

"Not a fair hunt at all," he went on. "I think if I find her, I'll set her running and finish her fast. I'm not into the kinky stuff."

I had a sudden feeling of revulsion. This was a bright and talented woman he was talking about, someone whom I had grown to care about. It was time to put the clown to sleep. I casually dropped my hand to my pocket for the taser. Up close he was a big man, bordering on the massive, and I hoped it would have the power to bring him to his knees.

Time for some honesty. The cardinal had asked me to try and do all this without loss of life. I had not made any promises. It would have been easy to take out the target pistol and put a double tap into Dorf's grinning skull. He might not have been a killer — yet — but he was a vile man, and I didn't think the world would be a worse place for his removal. But I am a vain man, and it appealed to my vanity to accept the challenge of rescuing Magda without bloodshed. And besides, the gun would have made too much noise. That was probably the real reason I went for the taser.

He was smiling vacantly at me, and then he wasn't.

It happened so fast. One second he was standing there with that goofy look. The next, there was a slight twitch of his hip and a fist the size of a ham was heading towards my face with the accuracy and force of an Exocet missile.

I ducked. Or at least my eyes signalled to my brain to react, and my brain sent the instructions to my muscles. But by the time all that neural activity had happened, I had run out of time. In other words, I knew I should duck. But I didn't. The ham hit me in the nose, and fireflies danced in front of my eyes, and I went down like a fallen log.

Rookie mistake. I should never have been within range of a fist. As I fell towards the steel floor, I retained enough wit to tuck my head in, staring at my navel. Old martial art trick — your head doesn't snap back and hit the floor. As soon as I hit the deck, I lifted my legs and tucked them into my chest, then continued the movement. The momentum of his punch helped. My legs passed over my head and I back-rolled onto my feet, about eight feet away from Dorf. My head was still groggy, and I let instincts guide my movements. My hands came up in a defensive criss-cross in front of my face, and my left foot slid forward to give a side-on target.

I shook my head to clear it, and the fireflies flitted away. I didn't have time to watch their departure. Dorf charged at me, his fists swinging. He was like a charging rhino — big, clumsy, but fast.

In an emergency, my brain slows down and goes into distraction-free mode. No extraneous thoughts. I analysed what I knew so far. He had swung from the hip rather than the shoulder. That's why I had missed the punch. A boxer will raise his fists before punching. So you get some indication it's on its way. A punch from the hip is more martial arts than boxing. Karate, taekwondo, or kickboxing? The main difference is how they use their feet, and once you know that, you know how to defend against their feet.

I got no clue. He was on me and punching, fists in a furious flurry. I swayed and bobbed, taking as many of the punches as I could on my arms and shoulders. They weren't doing damage, but they were hurting. A lot.

The fight did not last long. He was good. Fitter than he looked, and as strong as a bull. And his hands were surprisingly fast. But I had seen it all before. He had an orthodox stance — left foot forward, leading with a jab to set up the powerful right hand. I stepped to his right and his jab missed me by a wide margin. He moved his right foot around to his left, then lifted his left foot to move into a better punching position. As his left foot came back down, I shuffled forward and swept it out from under him with a vicious kick. He yelled in surprise and went down on one knee. Before he could right himself, I drove my knee into his face, hard. I heard the satisfying sound of bone crunching as his nose crumpled into his face. He went over backwards and hit the ground, limp.

I was taking no chances. I fell to the ground after him, hitting him in the face with my elbow. Overkill.

I sat beside him and checked for a pulse. Strong. Then I took a quick look at his nose. He wouldn't breathe through it for a while, and sneezing would be agony once he woke up. But he would live. One down, and by the cardinal's rules.

I went MacGyver on him. I began by removing his boots and stripping his laces. I tied his feet together, and pulled the knot so tight nothing short of a knife was going to open it. Then I tied his trussed feet to the railing of the walkway. I then did the same to his hands. Finally I removed his two socks, tied them together, and put the knot in his mouth. I tied the other ends of the socks around the back of his head. I did it carefully. He would be able to breathe, but not to talk. He was secure until our game was over.

I sat back and surveyed my work, pleased with myself. I was feeling a bit smug.

Then I heard a voice.

FORTY-EIGHT

"Bravo!"

There was a small ironic round of applause. I spun fast.

Strubel was leaning casually against the railing, smiling at me. But there was nothing casual about the target pistol in his hand, aimed squarely at my head. His hand was rock steady, and the barrel was unwavering.

Slowly I straightened up, keeping my movements relaxed. I didn't want to spook him. He was a jerky bastard at the best of times, always twitching and quivering. Not good when his finger was on a trigger.

"How are you doing, Johannes? Enjoying the game?"

"Loving it. Two of my opponents are eliminated already."

I felt a quiver of excitement. *Two?* "Have you taken Angie out?"

He smiled. "Not yet. But you have taken our friend Dorf out, and now you are out. Two down, one to go."

I looked at him. He looked at me.

"I know what you're thinking," he said. "You're wondering if I drop my hand and lose my concentration, can you take me? I'll give you the answer. I am deliberately four metres away from you. No matter what you do, I have plenty of time to bring up my gun and put a round in your face. Understand?"

"Understand. But do you really want to take this that seriously? It's a game."

He shook his head. "Tonight I'm going to kill one of the most famous women on the planet. I won't pretend it will be the first life I have taken, but it will be the first I've taken purely for fun. When I kill her, I'll be stepping over a line. You really think your death will prey on my mind?"

I shrugged. He had me there. Unless…

"Fair enough," I said. "Let's get it over with. My gun is tucked into my belt, and the safety is on. I'm going to remove it with my left hand and lower it to the floor, then slide it across the floor to you."

"There really is no need for that," he said. "I can just shoot you and remove your gun once you bleed out."

"And give up your advantage?"

That got him. He looked puzzled.

"If you shoot me," I explained, "Angie will hear the shot. And she'll know where you are. And she's a hell of a lot scarier than me."

He thought about it, then nodded. "Okay, take out your gun slowly, and slide it across to me."

He had a big grin on his face, like a school bully taking lunch money off a smaller kid. Moving slowly so as not to spook him, I lifted open my jacket with my right hand, then took the gun carefully by the butt with my left, and pulled it from my belt. Holding it with my fingertips, I lowered it to the floor. Straightening up, I shoved it towards him with my foot.

"Very good," he said. "Now I bend down to pick up the gun, and you jump me."

Yes. That was the plan. Apparently less brilliant than I thought.

"The taser is in my jacket pocket," I said, speaking as if I hadn't been interrupted. "I'll lower that to the floor too."

He leaned back, one hand resting casually on the wall of the generator, the other holding the target pistol loosely by his side, but ready for an instant hip shot. I had one roll of the dice left.

Slowly I reached into my pocket and pulled out the taser. "I'm going to lower it to the floor, and slide it along to you, like I did with the pistol. You win this round. I'd just like to point out one thing. You don't actually have to kill me. You could taser me and tie me up, like I tied up Dorf."

"Very true," he said. "But where would be the fun in that?"

With the gun in his hand, he gestured to me to hurry up. Yeah, like that was going to happen. I knew a sudden movement would cost me my life. So I moved with calm leisureliness.

I reached into my pocket and gripped the taser. Then I removed it from my pocket. I looked him straight in the eye. When you look a man in the eye, he looks you in the eye. Natural reaction. And when a man is looking you in the eye, he is not looking at your hand.

Still moving with painful slowness, I touched the stun gun to the wall of the generator and pressed the trigger. Instantly 100,000 volts shot through the metallic shell of the machine. The stream of electrons moved at close to the speed of light, crossing the four metres that separated me from Strubel in a nanosecond. Distance diminished the force of the charge somewhat but enough got through, sending a powerful electric current through Strubel's fingers into his body.

His arm convulsed as he jerked away from the metal, breaking the charge. For a fraction of a second his neural pathways had gone into overload. He quickly regained control over his body, but by that stage I had covered the distance between us and smashed into him at speed. Like a rugby tackle I drove on through him, shoving his body in front of me. We hit the railing, and I reached between his legs, grabbing his belt. Then I straightened up and lifted him off the ground, pushing him backwards over the railing. There was a moment

233

of resistance, then his body passed the tipping point. I let go, and watched as he crashed to the ground twenty feet below.

I took my time getting down to him. He wasn't going anywhere. When I reached him, he was semi-conscious and moaning. His shoulder was distorted badly. Without an x-ray I couldn't be sure, but it looked broken rather than dislocated to me. The screaming he did when I tied his arms behind his back with his laces confirmed my diagnosis. I gagged him with his socks next — a thing I wish I had done first — and finished by securing his feet.

"You were right — two down," I said to him. Then I smashed the butt of his pistol into the side of his head, viciously. His eyes rolled up, and I knew I wouldn't be hearing from him for several hours.

FORTY-NINE

She wasn't in the generating room. That was obvious. I could have searched the whole place, but that would have been wasting time. If Angie was there, she would have taken advantage of my fight with Strubel and put an arrow between my shoulders.

Strubel had made the amateur mistake of talking instead of just shooting me. She wouldn't. Of that I was sure.

Even though I knew she wasn't in the generating room, I still had to check it thoroughly. Not to have done so would have been acting like a rookie. And also, it was a bit of a salvage hunt. I began by taking Dorf's knife. I thought of taking his pistol, but instead ejected the clip and slipped it in my pocket. Without a clip, the target pistol was no longer a weapon. I also took Strubel's clip. I thought of taking his crossbow, but decided against it. Who uses an arrow when you have a gun? Only a moron.

Feeling like Rambo, I quickly went through the building, and in ten minutes I was happy that Magda was not there. Neither was Angie. Time to move on.

Before leaving the generating room, I scavenged a few more things that might or might not help me during the rest of the night. In a canteen room off the main floor I found an old plastic coke bottle. It gave me an idea, so I found one of the toilets. There was an old bog roll and I pulled off a dozen metres of tissue, stuffing them into my pocket. Then I crushed the bottle and put it in with the tissue. Time to move on to the next room.

I had one advantage over Angie. I had known that the game was going to be played in an abandoned power station. Knowing that, I had studied the layout as best I could. The main building was clear, and could be abandoned. That left the storage area, and the administrative building.

Instinct told me that if Magda wasn't in the generating room, she would be in the administrative block. Counterintuitively, I decided to ignore the administrative block and check out the warehouses. The reason was simple: I didn't want to rescue Magda until Angie Koll was out of the game.

I found a door. It opened on to a yard. If I went left, I rounded a corner and approached the side of the administrative block. If I moved straight ahead, I'd hit the first warehouse. If I turned right, I would end up in the parking lot. I looked left and right, then crossed the yard to the warehouse complex. I took a deep breath before pushing the door open and stepping through.

The room was faintly illuminated by moonlight pouring through the skylights overhead and through the windows. But shadows danced on the edge of my peripheral vision.

I walked about two metres into the room, then dropped to one knee.

As I did, I heard a twang and hiss as an arrow passed over my head, missing me by a whisker. Had I been standing, it would have thudded into my chest and the game would have come to a disappointing end.

FIFTY

I looked up in time to see a figure retreating behind a stack of pallets.

I don't know what instinct had caused me to duck once I entered the room. I think I was just thinking like an assassin. I had been the one hiding behind the door often enough. I knew Angie was a killer. So I had her behaviour nailed. Or maybe I had subconsciously caught a whiff of her perfume?

"Good shot," I shouted. She didn't reply. She wasn't going to make any amateur mistakes. But I did have one thing going for me. She didn't know I had already taken two players out of the game. She believed it was necessary to kill me silently rather than betray her position. That was why she had chosen the arrow, rather than the target pistol. That was why I was still alive.

I moved into cover myself, behind a bin to the side of the door. The bin wouldn't provide any more protection than a T-shirt against a Magnum round. But against the .22 from the target pistol, or against her arrows, I was safe. To get me she would have to move. To ascertain my new position, she would have to show her head.

I waited. So did she. She had the patience of a hunter. Ten full minutes passed. Neither of us were in a hurry. We were only an hour into the game and there were two hours left. She moved first, as I knew she would. She hunted for fun, while I hunted for money. If she failed, she had a bad day; but if I failed, I didn't eat. And I might get killed. So however good she thought she was, I was better.

Her head appeared around the far side of the stack of pallets. It was all I needed. I removed the crushed coke bottle from my pocket and lobbed it across the room. It clattered and skittered across the floor. Instantly, she stepped out from cover and faced the noise, her bow raised and an arrow in the notch. The bow was drawn.

I saw the brief look of confusion in her face as she realised she was facing nothing, then I stood and in one smooth movement I threw Dorf's hunting knife at her.

Here's the thing about hunting knives. They are designed for skinning your kill, and for gutting it before you toss it on the grill. They are good in a knife fight. But they are less effective than a box of eggs as a throwing weapon. A throwing knife is completely different from a hunting knife. The handle is smaller, and the blade and handle are balanced carefully so that it flies point first into its target. So I knew as I launched the knife that it was not going to cause significant injury.

I could have used the pistol, but I was still trying to play by the cardinal's rules. *Bring 'em in alive.* I wasn't wedded to the idea, but I would try.

So I threw the knife, regarding it more as a baseball pitch than a lethal attack. The weapon flew through the air. Simultaneously, Angie turned towards me and brought the bow up, pulling back the string. I began to drop down and to the side. It was a race. Three runners and the outcome still in the air.

The knife won. It bounced off her forehead, leaving a deep cut. From the look of the wound, I would guess the heavy handle hit her. It would need stitches, and she would have a headache tomorrow. But no real harm done.

Second and third place in the race didn't matter. I hit the floor safely, so I claim second. And as the knife struck her face,

Angie let go of the taut string of the bow. The arrow twanged out in a shallow downwards trajectory, struck the floor and bounced up, before embedding itself in the door I had walked through ten minutes earlier.

I scrambled to my feet and charged at her. She lost precious time wiping at the blood streaming down her face, then she fumbled for another arrow. But I was on her at that stage. I barrelled into her, throwing her to the ground and stumbling on top of her.

She had the arrow out, and she slashed viciously at my throat with the point. But an arrow is not a slashing weapon. It is a stabbing weapon. It hurt a lot as the point raked across my exposed throat, but it didn't break the skin. I punched her in the face and felt the blood on my knuckles.

Just then a door opened and a man stepped into the room. He was holding a flashlight. He shone it right at us, and I closed my eyes so that I wouldn't lose my precious night vision. Then he moved it away again. I looked up. It was one of my two muggers. He was obviously on patrol duty. I had only seen the two muggers and Rodriguez from the beginning of the game. It looked like he was operating with a skeleton staff. Good to know for what was to come later.

"Sorry," he said. "Just checking on things. I didn't mean to disturb the game. Carry on." Then he turned and left the room. The door with the arrow embedded in it closed, but I didn't hear it click. He had left it slightly ajar.

I was brought back to the reality of my situation when Angie struck me again. But this time she had realised that an arrow does not slash. She stabbed viciously into my left shoulder, and I felt a searing pain as the point of the arrow penetrated my jacket, my skin, and then the muscles beneath it. She drove it in nearly six centimetres.

The pain was intense, but I forced myself not to pull away. Instead of trying to jerk my shoulder out of the embrace of the arrow, I leaned into it, and twisted my torso slightly. That made it difficult for her to yank out the arrow and stab again.

Then I slammed the heel of my right hand into her face, feeling the crunch as her nose smashed and flattened. Her head slammed back and the back of her skull bounced off the floor. I hit her again, and felt no resistance from her neck muscles. She was out cold.

Quickly, I trussed her like I had trussed the others, then retrieved the knife and used it to score a deep nick in the bow. I put the bow against the wall and stood on it, snapping it. I knew she was out of the game, but anything can happen, and if she escaped she would no longer have her preferred weapon. Her pistol was tucked into her belt above the right hip, and I felt a bit pervy removing it. I stripped out the clip and put it in my pocket with the others. I now had enough bullets to start a war against a small nation. I was about to fling away her gun, when I put it in my jacket pocket. I don't know why.

I took a moment to consider my options, then searched the floor until I retrieved the coke bottle. I blew into it to straighten it out, then removed the sheets of toilet paper from my pocket and balled them up, dropping them one at a time into the bottle until it was loosely filled. Then I jammed the barrel of my pistol into the bottle and stood up. Rambo might have sneered at me, but MacGyver would have been proud.

I walked to the door and stepped out into the night.

FIFTY-ONE

The yard facing me looked empty. I knew better.

"I got her," I said loudly. "I know you were looking. You might as well come out."

He was grinning when he walked around the corner of the warehouse and approached me. It was the man who had disturbed Angie and me during our struggle. I knew he had watched the fight through a chink in the door, because he had not closed it fully when he left the room. It is human nature to stay and watch. I would have been stunned if he was not still in the vicinity.

"You did a number on her alright," he said. "I'm glad I didn't have money on the fight, because I would have put it on her. She really hated you. That was obvious all day."

"Tell me about it," I muttered. "She's ripped my shoulder asunder." I looked at the blood streaming down my arm, then back at the mugger. Let's call him Mugger Number Two, because he was the guy who drove the getaway motorcycle, rather than the guy who attacked me in the woods. That guy was, unsurprisingly, Mugger Number One in my head. We would meet again, soon. "I don't know whether you know yet, but I have taken out the other two players too."

He raised an eyebrow. "I'm impressed."

"So now I'm the last man standing," I went on. "Can you tell me where Magda is being held?"

He smiled and shook his head. "That's not how this works. You still have to find her. No clues."

"I was afraid of that," I sighed.

There are two ways of extracting information from an unwilling witness — aside from subterfuge and trickery. The methods are the carrot and the stick. The stick is beating, intimidation, and torture. It is guaranteed to get you information, and often quite quickly. The problem is the quality of the information. If you are torturing someone properly, he will tell you anything to end the pain. He will tell what he thinks you want to hear, rather than what you actually need to hear. I have found torture extremely effective, and extremely unreliable, which is why I never use it anymore. Fool me once, shame on you. Fool me twice, shame on me.

The carrot method is far more effective. Just find the right encouragement, and your witness will spill the beans and feel good about it. Sometimes you appeal to their vanity, or their greed, or their sense of right and wrong. The annals of espionage are filled with spies who acted out of a warped sense of patriotism or decency. It can sometimes take a while to find the right carrot, but it is always worth the effort.

I decided to use a carrot on Mugger Number Two.

I smiled as I lifted the coke bottle and aimed the end of it at his torso.

"What's that?" he asked. "I saw you making it."

"It's a homemade sound suppressor, a sort of silencer for a gun," I explained. "A target pistol doesn't make much noise, but it makes some. And if I fire it, people will know. But with the silencer, I can use the gun and nobody but you and I will know. Here — let me show you."

I pulled the trigger, and listened with pleasure to the slight pop. I watched as Mugger Number Two gasped, clutched his stomach, stumbled, and sat down clumsily on the ground. He lifted his hands away from his shirt and saw that they were covered in blood. His face went pale, and he moaned.

I moved fast. I didn't want him to pass out before we had a chance to chat. Gripping him under the shoulders, I dragged him across the ground and into the warehouse, where the unconscious Angie was breathing heavily. I propped him up against the wall and tied his feet together. Then I cut the sleeve from his shirt and bundled it against the ragged wound about five centimetres above his navel. The blood seemed very dark, but that could have been the poor light.

I pushed his hand against the crumpled sleeve and told him to keep the pressure on.

Where was the carrot in my approach, you might wonder? I was about to lay it out for him.

"Keep that cloth pressed into the wound. You don't want to risk bleeding out," I said, trying to make my voice sympathetic and comforting.

"You bastard — you shot me!" he said. He wasn't buying the sympathy.

"I know," I said. "And I am sorry. It's not something I wanted to do. I didn't wake up this morning and say, you know, today would be a good day to shoot a man in the gut. But you left me no choice. If you had told me where Magda was being held, I wouldn't have had to shoot you. So let's start over again. Where is he holding her?"

"Fuck you!" He spat the words out.

"I am going to be straight with you," I said, still smiling. "I entered this hunt under false pretences. I am not here to kill Magda, but to save her. I'm trying not to kill anyone, including you. You saw me not killing Angie. I could have, but I didn't. I could have killed you, but I didn't. That's the good news.

"The bad news is you might still die. It's up to you. I want to help you, but you have to help me."

The carrot.

"You see, I shot you in the stomach. A .22 doesn't have much stopping power. But you don't need stopping power if you shoot a guy in the gut. The bullet will have ripped a hole in the wall of your stomach, and the contents are now leaking into your body cavity. You're facing a slow and painful death from blood poisoning and toxic shock. If you get immediate medical aid, you can be put on strong antibiotics to control the raging infections that already have begun to eat into your organs. And the hole in your stomach can be stitched closed.

"You have about two hours. After that, all doctors will be able to do is reduce your pain for your final few hours.

"So here's your choice. Tell me where Magda is and I will rescue her, then call in a doctor for you. Or don't tell me, and I will waste time looking for her before I call in a doctor. If I even bother. Spill the beans, you live. Don't spill, you die."

"Fuck you."

"Just to make this more interesting, I rolled my bullets in rat droppings at the start of the hunt. You have a fascinating mix of bacteria multiplying inside you. But make the right decision and make it quickly, and in a few weeks you'll be right as rain."

What a carrot — it would beat any stick. It had to.

The rat dropping story was not true. I made it up to sell the carrot. But it was a good story — I filed it away in case I ever needed it for real.

I sat back and waited for Mugger Number Two to see the light. It didn't take long for him to switch from *Fuck You* to *Please Help Me*.

"She's in a crawl space above the manager's office, in the administrative building. Fourth room on the left."

"And Rodriguez?"

"He's not in that office."

Of course not. It would be too obvious.

"Where is he?"

He hesitated for a moment. Beads of sweat were forming on his forehead, and his skin was already beginning to take on a greyish hue. Finally, it came.

"He's in the second office on the right. With Miguel."

Who was Miguel? Had to be Mugger Number One. I had a score to settle with him as well. I stood. It had been easy in the end.

"You'll call a doctor?" he pleaded.

"Would I lie to you?" I replied.

FIFTY-TWO

Sneaking up on Rodriguez was very easy. I just walked up to the administrative building, walked in the main door, walked down the corridor, and pushed open the second door on the left. No sneakiness, no subterfuge. It was all part of the game, and no room was off limits to us. That had been made clear during our instructions.

So I just walked into the room, spotted Rodriguez and Miguel — whom I recognised immediately as Mugger Number One — and grinned stupidly.

"Last place," I said. "She's not in the generating plant, and she's not in the storage area. So she must be here. Am I wrong?"

Rodriguez looked at me and smiled. "You know I can't tell you that, Mr Allen. But you are welcome to search the office. Have you seen any of your fellow competitors in the past hour?"

I was pretty sure he had us all under surveillance, at least partially. So I answered honestly.

"I've bumped into a few of them. I believe I am the last man standing."

"If that's true, well done you. But it's not about being the last man standing. It's about finding the target. I hope you didn't kill any of them. I don't want problems tomorrow morning."

"Don't worry. They are all safe. The only thing you will have to deal with are sour grapes."

I moved casually into the room, and took off my jacket, tossing it onto the desk in front of Rodriguez. The gun in the pocket clunked against the wood. The butt protruded a little.

Angie's gun. I ignored it and took a chair opposite Rodriguez. I looked at Mugger Number One and said: "A coffee please. Milk, no sugar."

He glared daggers at me and didn't move. But Rodriguez looked at him and nodded slightly. Not looking happy, he stepped past me and left the room.

Rodriguez laughed. "He doesn't like you."

"As long as he doesn't spit in the coffee."

I relaxed. I was confident. Rodriguez was alert, but I didn't think he suspected he was in any danger. I wasn't quite ready to tackle him yet, though. I needed to get Mugger Number One out of the picture.

He came back after a few minutes, with a mug in one hand. I stood to take the mug from him, and as he handed it over, he had to move towards me. As he did, I took a step towards him and suddenly snapped my head forward.

The human head weighs a good ten kilos and is surrounded by a hard shell of bone. It's a magnificent computing machine, it's a great place to hang a hat, but it is also a potential weapon, overlooked by most people. The headbutt, also known as the Glasgow Handshake, hurts the giver a little. But it hurts the receiver a lot more. You just have to ensure that the right part of your head connects with the wrong part of their head, and it is lights out, show over.

Mugger Number One fell back against the wall, then bounced back towards me. I stepped in and drove my knee up into his groin, then watched him fall, the mug of coffee shattering on the floor and the brown liquid pooling. I kicked him in the head for good measure, then turned towards Rodriguez.

He was on his feet in a shooter's stance, the dark barrel of a gun aimed firmly at my slightly stinging forehead.

I froze. "Oh shit!" I muttered.

Then I looked down at the table. The gun that had slipped from my jacket pocket was gone. It was Angie's gun that was pointing at me.

"Oh shit!" I muttered again.

"Oh shit indeed, Mr Allen," he said. He had a tight smile on his face. "And you were playing the game so well. All you had to do was finish your search, find the target, and have your fun."

I shrugged. "What are you going to do with me?"

"You have broken the rules. I might kill you. I would be within my rights." His finger tightened on the trigger.

"Before you do, I think there is something you should know. I am going to move my hands very slowly. Please try not to shoot me."

I did as I promised. Very slowly I lifted my hands to my head, and pulled off my red wig, dropping it to the floor. It landed in the spilled coffee. Damn. Thank God it was from a friend rather than hired, because I wasn't going to get a deposit back on it now. I peeled off the goatee, but left the scar in place. I'd got kinda fond of it. It gave me the rakish look of a pirate. Finally, I dropped the Cornish accent.

I smiled at him. "It's me, Victor."

The look on his face was priceless. A mix of confusion, fury, and a small hint of fear, which disappeared quickly.

"Bet you didn't expect that now," I laughed. "We are back working together, you and I, trying to save Magda's life."

He shook his head. "Hardly that."

I dropped my hands casually and put them in my jacket pocket. I was trying to look as nonchalant as possible.

"Who do you have with you?" he asked.

"I came alone," I replied.

I could see the thoughts flickering across his face. Finally he said: "Yes, I can see you being arrogant enough to come without backup. You know what they say: doctors bury their mistakes. But hitmen are buried by theirs. You should not have come alone. By the way, what did you do with the real Mr Allen?"

"Reggie was working with us right from the start. In fact, we even identified this hunt site in advance, so I had an advantage over my fellow hunters. It was a clever twist to get rid of us all in the demolition explosion in the morning. The only question we have is — were you planning on dying in the explosion yourself? The cardinal said you would do that. It would be your final act. I said you would walk away and kill again. Settle our dispute before you kill me, please?"

"I think I will let you die without knowing." He raised the gun.

"One little thing," I said. "I've taken care of the other three competitors. So I have more than one gun. I kept two of the guns. You have one now. I have the other in my jacket pocket. I'm aiming from the hip, but it's close range. I think I can still shoot well enough to kill you."

"You might shoot well enough, but can you shoot fast enough?" His finger was tightening.

"Let's make it interesting," I said. "I'll count to three, like an old-fashioned duel. At three, we both shoot. Let the better man, or the luckier man, win."

I smiled my most winning smile. I was playing the odds. He was a very egotistical man. He would not back down from the challenge.

He smiled, and nodded slightly. But he didn't lower the gun.

"One," I said.

Time seemed to expand. The word seemed elongated in my mind. Sounds seemed to recede.

"Two," I said.

Almost in action replay slo-mo, I could see his mouth twitch up, his eyes crinkle in a look of amusement, his fingers tightening, the barrel steadying…

Then he pulled the trigger. Before three.

Instead of a muzzle flash, there was a hollow click. His face froze, then he pulled the trigger twice more. Two more clicks.

"You've got Angie's gun," I said. "I removed the clip when I took it off her. I did that to all the target pistols. All except one. The one in my pocket. I think I can make the shot."

I took a breath and let it out, then said: "Three."

I pulled the trigger in my jacket pocket. Shooting from the hip is never easy, but I had put in my time at the range. I was delighted with the result. My aim was true. The bullet ripped a hole in my jacket — that would go on expenses at the end. It continued across the short two-metre distance, then met flesh, easily ripping through the soft tissue, shattering bone.

I watched in satisfaction as Rodriguez's gun fell from his powerless grip. He stared in horror at the bloody mess that had been his elbow.

"You know my brief. I was told to bring you in alive."

Then I removed my gun from my pocket and carefully took my next shot, blowing out his kneecap, dropping him to the ground.

EPILOGUE

There is not much more to tell.

Magda was where I was told she would be. She was in a small attic — more a crawlspace really — above the manager's office, the fourth room on the left. I put a chair on the desk and gained access. She cowered away when she heard me approach, but once she realised who it was, she clung to me like a limpet.

I got her down eventually, and was putting my jacket on her when she spotted the blood from my shoulder wound. That brought another flood of tears. For a while I let her hold on to me. She needed the security. But eventually I had to prise her free. I made strong, sweet tea in Rodriguez's office. Tied to a chair, he snarled at me, but with his knee and elbow blown out there was not much else he could do. I brought the tea back to Magda, and as she drank it I used my small bum phone to call Benoluchi. He in turn called in the cavalry, saying he had got an anonymous tip about Magda's whereabouts.

Then I got out of there, fast.

It was difficult to leave Magda. Partially because she was very traumatised, and didn't want to let me go. Partially because my shoulder stung like a bitch. I was in agony. But I pulled myself away and got out, making my way to the hills at the rear of the generating station. It would have been easier to go out the front, but I didn't want to walk past the police cars that were rushing to the scene.

I was in a cold sweat by the time I had reached a small country road about a kilometre away. By that time, the plant was lit up like Christmas. I turned towards Leon and began the five-kilometre walk into the town. It took an hour and a half.

When I walked into the hotel, there was an impromptu party going on. Magda was sitting with her camera crew and Fermin Benoluchi. They were happy but subdued. There were clear signs of exhaustion on all sides, and Magda knew she would face a day of police interviews once she woke up the next morning.

Fermin spotted me and beckoned me over. "The police are gone," he whispered. "You missed them by ten minutes."

When I pulled off my jacket, he was horrified by the mess of my shoulder. He wanted to rush me to a hospital, then he wanted to call a doctor. As I could not explain an arrow wound without admitting my involvement in the evening's activities, I demurred. Eventually, we reached a compromise acceptable to all. He called in a vet that the local bishop — annoyed to be woken up in the wee hours, even by a cardinal — recommended.

The vet was efficient but not very gentle. He cleaned the wound and stitched it roughly. "It will do for now," he muttered, "but there is tendon damage. You'll need to get it sorted out by a surgeon."

He offered me a shot of ketamine, a strong horse tranquiliser. Luckily he adjusted the dosage, and I went to bed floating on a cloud of bliss. I was just drifting off when my door opened softly. Someone entered, and Magda slipped lithely between my sheets.

"I need to be held," she said.

So I held her, and fell asleep in her warm embrace.

I woke at noon the following day, and my bed was empty. She had slipped out early, and just as softly slipped out of my life.

Whatever spark there was between us had ignited into nothing more than a cuddle. Still, I could fantasise…

I heard some time later that she had gone home to Poland after the investigation, but had returned to Spain a month later and completed the entire Camino privately, on foot. It took her five weeks, and she claimed that the experience had changed her. She then returned to the porn industry.

So it was just Fermin who joined me for lunch on my final day. He was looking unnaturally chirpy. It had all come up roses for him. The Camino Killer was caught. Magda was safe. And she was off the Camino, so the Church no longer had to deal with an adult actress treading holy ground.

"This calls for champagne," he suggested.

"Not a good mix with ketamine," I responded.

He insisted on choosing lunch. "Galicia is famous for pulpo — grilled octopus. We are not in Galicia yet, but you can't leave the Camino without trying it."

I was reluctant. I've had octopus before, and it is like eating the grilled inner tubes of bicycles. But Fermin was right; this was succulent and flavourful. Just before the plates arrived, he slipped an envelope across the table to me.

"Receipt for the bank transfer," he explained. "I added an extra 5,000 euros as a thank you. You took some very evil characters off the streets. We do appreciate that. I believe all people are capable of repenting and redeeming themselves, but I am very happy that the hunters will seek their redemption behind bars. Probably best for the rest of the world." Then he smiled. "And you did it without killing anyone. That's the real reason for the bonus. My conscience is clear. I picked the right man."

I was curious. "How did you find me?"

He tapped his nose mischievously. "The Vatican may be changing, but we still have our little black book of contacts. Talking of contacts, why don't you ring your brother?" He looked at me. "Now," he added.

Feeling a little like a schoolboy in the presence of the principal, I did make the call.

"Eliot — how's it hanging?" came the cheery voice of my brother Lester. "What part of the world are you ringing from?"

My bloody pretence of being an adventure tour operator.

"I'm in Leon."

"I thought the Camino would be a bit tame for you."

Sharp. A week ago, I had barely heard of the Camino. He knew the cities along the route.

"A bit of R & R. Listen, I'm ringing about your trip to Morocco. Who the hell is Serena?"

There was a pause, then he said: "Who do you think Serena is? You've known her for years." That didn't help. His next words shocked me. "She's my wife, you moron."

"You're married to Chloe."

"Yes." There was a big dramatic sigh on the other end of the line. "Did you not read my Christmas email?"

"Of course I read it." I tried to keep the guilt out of my voice. I hadn't read it. Not a word. I had replied, but in vague platitudes. Who reads Christmas emails? They are just so much fluff about how well the other person is doing and cute stories about pets and children. No thanks.

"I'll remind you," he said, in a tone of exaggerated patience. "Chloe has finally got her Equity card. You remember she always wanted to act?"

Vaguely.

"Well, now she can. But there was already a Chloe Locke on the Equity books, so she had to pick a different professional name. She's switched to her middle name. Serena Locke. It was all in the email."

"Yes, I remember now," I lied.

"No, you don't," he said. "But we'll let it go. Have you organised that mountain thing for me?"

Now I sighed. "Chloe — Serena — has never climbed a mountain in her life. What makes her want to do one now?"

"She said she wanted to revisit Morocco. We went there for our honeymoon. And she said she wanted to do something exciting this time."

Putting a woman like Chloe — Serena — on a mountain was a recipe for divorce. But there were plenty of fun things to do in Morocco.

"Give me a few days," I said, and hung up.

Fermin was smiling at me. "The world is a good place. Try to remember that," he said.

I kept in touch with Fermin. I get an occasional Facebook message from Magda. That's how I know the rest. That, and a few newspaper accounts I came across. Victor Rodriguez was convicted of seven murders, and will never see an open field or a fashionable boulevard again. My three fellow hunters were convicted of attempted murder, and got sentences ranging from twelve years (Angie) to eighteen years (Strubel and Dorf). I think if the juries had got to know the hunters as well as I did, those sentences would have been quite a bit longer.

Mugger One and Mugger Two were also done, for attempted murder and for kidnapping. They each got twenty-two years. Though I appeared in a lot of the defence testimony at the trials, I was not called to testify, and Fermin and the police dismissed all accounts of a fourth hunter as a smokescreen created by the defence. I sent the prosecutor a bottle of Talisker for keeping me out of it.

That wraps the story up. Aside, of course, from the unspeakable Reginald Allen. What became of our Bangkok paedophile?

There I saw a side to Fermin I had not expected to see.

That final lunch in Leon, we followed the grilled pulpo with a goat's cheese cheesecake which was surprisingly good. Maybe not Baileys and chocolate cheesecake good, but good nonetheless. Then we had strong coffees. Then a shot of rum. Three shots, actually. I felt he was building up to something.

"I've kept Reggie Allen at a local monastery for the past two days. We need to let him go now," Fermin said. "I'd like it if you'd come with me."

Officially I was off his dime at that stage, but unofficially I liked him, so I agreed.

The monastery was a huge yellow sandstone building three minutes' walk outside the pedestrianised centre of Leon. One side was a pilgrim hostel, while the second entrance led to a cheap but cheerful pilgrim hotel. Bigger rooms, single occupancy, showers en suite, but most importantly, no curfew and no eight a.m. checkout. Allen was in one of the rooms in the hotel area, and Fermin had the key.

When we knocked and let ourselves in, he looked relieved to see us. I think the isolation was getting to him. I was surprised that he was bearing it all so patiently. I supposed — rightly as it turned out — that Bill was handling some problems back in Bangkok as a sort of quid pro quo. But he felt he had done his bit, earned Bill's favour, and now just wanted to go home.

Fermin sat down on his bed. "Reggie, I know I promised you a flight back to Bangkok once this was over, but I'd like you to consider taking a month out to attend a clinic we have in Rome. It could help you with your … urges." Fermin's face creased when he said it, but he pushed on. "I have arranged for a top specialist to work with you for the next month — at our expense. All you have to do is say the word, and we fly you to Rome tonight."

Allen's lips twitched in a sneer. "Thank you for the kind offer, Padre, but I think I'll just head back east. I am quite happy with my urges the way they are."

I watched a look I didn't quite understand cross Fermin's face, then his face hardened with resolve.

"Very well. That was our deal. We will drive you to the airport."

Allen grinned and stood from the chair by the bed.

"But first," said Fermin, "my colleague here is going to castrate you. I am a cardinal of the Catholic church. I know the rap we've received in the past two decades, and there is no way I can add to that bad reputation by letting you walk out of here without trying to help you. We have let down enough children."

Allen went pale, but with fury rather than fear. He strode towards the door. I casually leaned against the plinth, blocking him. He stopped, and took a half-step back. "We had a deal," he said.

"And I am going to honour that deal. I will bring you to the airport. Once the bleeding stops," said Fermin. He reached into his pocket and took out a sharp scalpel. Then he took out a syringe. "We don't want it to hurt," he said.

I took a step forward, forcing Allen to step back towards the bed. I looked him in the eye and smiled. Sweat beaded on his brow.

It took less than a minute. It was interesting to watch a man's face as he mentally collapsed. After 38 seconds — by my estimate — he turned to Fermin.

"I'll go to Rome," he whispered.

As we left the hotel, Fermin gripped my elbow.

"Thanks for coming with me. I couldn't have done that on my own."

"What was in the syringe?" I asked.

"Water. I was banking on him taking the non-surgical option."

"And do you think the treatment will work?"

Fermin shrugged. "We have done enough evil, you and I, this past week. Some good had to come of all this. Yes, I think the treatment will work. I am an optimist."

I grinned and slapped him on the shoulder. "I think you are right," I said.

I am a cynic, and a liar.

A NOTE TO THE READER

Dear Reader,

Thank you for taking the time to read the second Eliot Locke thriller. An even bigger thanks if you have read the first too! They are great fun to write, and I hope that comes across to you. One of my favourite authors is Raymond Chandler, and in his essay 'The Simple Art of Murder' he described the perfect hero: "He must be a complete man and a common man and yet an unusual man. He must be, to use a rather weathered phrase, a man of honour, by instinct, by inevitability, without thought of it, and certainly without saying it. He must be the best man in his world and a good enough man for any world."

I don't know how well Eliot measures up to that, but he tries — or rather, I try to make him so. But no matter how hard you work on your character, he only comes alive when you put him in challenging and interesting situations. That is why I was so happy to take him on The Camino.

For several years my summer holidays have been spent walking sections of the various Camino routes into Santiago in northern Spain, with my good friend Dermot. I spend many hours plodding happily along, dreaming of my next morsel of delicious food, and thinking up situations to drop Eliot into. If my fellow pilgrims knew what unholy thoughts occupied my head, they would shudder to walk with me!

In a world getting safer and tamer by the year, the Camino is a little adventure that is open to all of us. Travel feeds the spirit and fuels the imagination. Especially travel that stretches beyond the boundaries of an apartment complex and a crowded swimming pool. I hope to take Eliot on many more travels. In the third instalment he will be in Moscow, and in the fourth a lot closer to home — because there is the exotic in the local too, if you look hard enough.

Nowadays, reviews by readers are essential to an author's success, so if you enjoyed the story the best way you can thank me is to take the few seconds required to post a review or rating on **Amazon** and **Goodreads**. I love hearing from readers, and you can connect with me through **my Facebook page**, via **Twitter**, or **through my website**.

Before I sign off, a few quick thank yous. Thank you to my editor Ronan O'Leary, a very talented filmmaker who is even more obsessive on grammar than I am. Thanks to my agent Isabel Atherton of Creative Writers, and to Amy Durant and all the staff at Sapere Books. Finally, but most importantly, thanks to Fr Hugh O'Dowd, an inspirational English teacher who turned a nerdish would-be physicist into a reader and writer. I will be forever grateful.

I hope we'll meet again in the pages of the next Eliot Locke adventure.

Dean Carson

www.deancarson.com

Sapere Books is an exciting new publisher of brilliant fiction and popular history.

To find out more about our latest releases and our monthly bargain books visit our website: **saperebooks.com**

Printed in Great Britain
by Amazon